THE CABOT GIRLS OF COVENTRY ISLAND

Geonn Cannon

Supposed Crimes LLC • Matthews, North Carolina

Fourteen Years Ago

THE SMALL *town on Coventry Island didn't have a name; it didn't
need one. Locals called it 'the town' or 'home,' and referring to the island
itself was as specific as they had to get. The streets bloomed out from the
ferry dock like tree branches. Restaurants and shops to the right, along the
south shore. Straight ahead was the heart of the town, the library and
church and grocery store. Take a left from the docks and you would see the
little town cemetery.*

*It was a sunny day, with a few clouds on the Canadian side of the
Strait of Juan de Fuca but otherwise clear. School had let out a few hours
ago and a swarm of kids were riding bikes down a side street on their way to
play in the woods. The ferry had just arrived. It was a small boat, not one of
the state's stylish fleet, and it waited patiently for the tourists currently on
the island to make their way down the hill and climb aboard for the return
trip to the mainland.*

*The first sign of trouble came in the form of a tall blonde girl striding
down the main road at a fast clip. She wasn't quite running but she was
obviously in a hurry. She trotted in such a way that people who saw her pass
by their storefronts came out to see whether she was running to something or
away from it. Ordinarily the three teenage girls pursuing her at a
meandering pace wouldn't be cause for alarm, but everyone recognized this
trio.*

They were the Cabot girls.

As the four girls continued down the street, the sky became dark.

Barty, the owner and captain of the boat, came off the bridge to look up at the suddenly ominous clouds building overhead. The blonde reached the dock and stopped running. Arwyn Cabot, the eldest, stopped. The twins followed her lead. Maeve looked sheepish. Cerys looked angry. The blonde was defiant but scared. The wind swept down the street like a broom, lifting the cloth of awnings and making grown men stumble a bit in surprise as they were shoved by unseen hands. The blonde girl on the dock was kicked back a few steps and put up a hand to protect her face.

"You can either leave on the boat or see how far you can swim," Arwyn said.

The blonde smiled incredulously. "You can't do this. You can't just kick me off the island!"

Cerys and Maeve lifted their hands in concert and the street was suddenly awash by a wall of rain. Barty ducked back into the safety of his ship and scrambled to put on his slicker. Waves kicked up and flooded the dock. Arwyn moved closer.

"You hurt my sisters. You did it deliberately and took great joy in what you were doing. Coventry Island doesn't need people like you."

Another wave crashed. This one was big enough to flood the lowest portion of the street. All three Cabot girls were soaked now, their faces shadowed by their hair, and even those witnesses who knew them well were suddenly frightened by what was happening. The sky growled... not thunder, but an actual rumbling groan which stretched from the far horizon until it was centered over the town.

The blonde turned and ran along the dock, covering her head in a futile attempt to protect herself from the rain. She clambered aboard and disappeared into the passenger section.

Once she was out of sight, the Cabots dropped their hands. The rain stopped, although evidence of the deluge still cascaded down the street. The Cabot girls remained where they were until the ferry was fully loaded. The woman who owned the bakery said she never even saw them blink. They certainly didn't shiver, even though their clothes were soaked through. Finally the ship pulled away from the dock and the girls relaxed.

When the ferry was gone, Arwyn Cabot turned and walked between her sisters. Cerys and Maeve turned and followed her. The three dripping Cabot girls, the latest generation of a family who had been on Coventry Island since its founding, marched single-file up the street through the center of town. The clouds dissipated as if they had never been there, though the cool breeze and scent of ozone still lingered. The renewed sun shone off puddles that had no right to exist.

In the days that followed, no one mentioned the scene. Soon enough it was all but forgotten. The people of Coventry Island were accustomed to weirdness when the Cabot family was involved, but drawing attention to it was just asking for trouble.

So no one spoke of it. No one wrote about it in the newspaper and gossips kept mum about the flash storm and the young woman who was forced off the island.

It was just easier that way.

CHAPTER ONE

EARLY EVENING transformed into full dark during the five minutes Arwyn Cabot was inside the store. She'd known the storm was brewing, of course, but she'd hoped her errands would be finished by the time it rolled in. No such luck on this trip. She stood for a minute under the awning and watched as the rain transformed the hard blacktop into a swirling expanse of oil. She breathed in deeply and smiled at the ozone and electricity in the air. There was nothing quite like a spring storm to invigorate her spirits.

Old Jonathan McCaulley was heading in and slowed down as he passed her. "Winnie, tell me you ain't goin' out on that boat when it's like this."

"Home is out there," Winnie said with a smile.

He slowed at the doorway of the store. "You and your sisters got plenty of firewood lined up for the winter?"

"We could always use more."

"You know where to find me." He pushed the door open and flooded the porch with golden light from within. "Be safe, Winnie! Home will still be there after the storm blows by."

She cinched the collar of her slicker and smiled at the older man. "I'll be fine, Mr. McCaulley. This storm and I have an understanding."

"Oh, well. Then that's okay then." He chuckled as he went into the safe and dry sanctuary. The door swung shut behind him.

Winnie took a moment to straighten her slicker while she was still protected by the building. She cinched the hood and tugged the zipper up as high as it would go, then ran to her truck. Her bags - brown paper inside white plastic - hung from her hands and bumped off her thighs as she splashed to where she had parked. Instead of fumbling with her keys she muttered a short phrase under her breath. The locks released with a barely audible "thunk!" She pulled the door open and dived inside.

Ideally she would have waited for a dry day to get groceries, but that wasn't really a viable option in this part of the state. Shield, Washington, was situated right on the edge of the Olympic Peninsula's rain shadow. Five miles east, it might be dry as a bone. But during the rainy season, Shield got rain three and a half weeks of rain out of every four. If she waited to get supplies, the cupboards would run bare, and there were some things a person just had to have.

She dug through the groceries and retrieved one of those essentials: a small bag of DuChilly hazelnuts roasted in rosemary. The nuts were unusually almond-shaped, salty and oily in equal measure, absolutely delicious. She didn't mind sharing with her sisters, but things were treasures meant to be enjoyed privately and clandestinely. It made the nuts taste even sweeter. She popped one into her mouth and chewed slowly as she watched the rain cascade down the windshield. The air rumbled in the atmosphere as the storm marched on, feeding the vast greenery and making wood look like polished stone.

Winnie ate another nut. She would allow herself three; that seemed like a fair number. She pushed it around with her tongue before setting it between her teeth and biting down. The boat was waiting for her at the dock, but she was running ahead of schedule. Barty, the skipper, would wait no matter what the weather did. She had time to savor, but she wasn't going to take advantage of his trust. She popped the last nut into her mouth and closed the bag so she wouldn't be tempted.

With her illicit snack finished, she twisted the key and groaned quietly as the engine rattled. She adjusted her grip on the steering wheel as if that would help and twisted the key again. Another rattle and a grind, then the relief when it came to life. She sighed and smiled, patted the dashboard, and hoped her luck held out long enough to get home.

"Good girl," she said out loud to the truck.

She drove through a seemingly abandoned town. Hers was the only vehicle on the street but the homes and businesses were so lit up that they looked like shadowboxes. She saw people within eating dinner, shopping, or standing at the glass to watch the rain sweep by. As expected, Barty and his boat were both waiting for her when she arrived. He waved as she pulled up the ramp and parked in the safe shell of the lower deck.

The boat swayed under her feet as she climbed to the main deck. She understood why people were reluctant to go out on the water during a storm, but she found it invigorating. They were never closer to nature than when they were caught in her grip from above and below. The sea and the wind joined into a single force and she was grateful to dance in their midst for just a little while, even if Barty was the one at the wheel.

He waved to her as he headed up to the bridge. "Ready to go home, Missus Cabot?"

"Every minute I'm away from it, Barty."

He grinned wide enough to show the missing teeth on either side of his mouth. Once he was safely on the bridge, Winnie pushed up the sleeves of her anorak and sweater as she crouched near the bow. She pressed her palms together, fingers bent slightly outward so they looked like two shells pressed back to back. Eyes closed, she rubbed her palms together and felt the energy pulling from deep within her. It curved around her shoulders and cascaded down to her elbows. By the time it reached her hands, the energy was raging as hard as the weather above them.

"Safe passage from your storms." She pressed her right hand to the deck and her left hand to the hull. She could feel the engine humming through the wood and the thin layer of rainwater between her and the vessel. "If it's within your grace to allow us protection, guide us safely home." When the prayer was finished she shook her hands before the pins and needles could set in. She looked up at the layers of heavy gray clouds and smiled.

Coventry Island - home - was just over a mile and a half from shore. Barty could cover the distance in just a few minutes, giving her just enough time to go inside and use the facilities. When she returned, the island loomed up ahead. She walked out onto the deck and pinched the hood of her slicker so the wind wouldn't push it off her head. Lines of little white and red houses clung to the rising slope of the land, as if some giant invisible hand was lifting the map to show off the quaint little town to new visitors.

Between the charcoal gray clouds and the gunmetal of the turbulent waves, beacons of light shone out from the dock in the form of five security lights that sparkled like miniature suns.

To the west she could see the sweep of the lighthouse warning away any ships passing them in the Strait. The pale beam passed over her and she felt like the land was welcoming her back into its embrace. She breathed in deeply once more and pushed her palms through the beads of rainwater that had accumulated on the railing. The energy of her family's home pushed in through her chest and warmed her heart, filled her with peace and happiness as Barty maneuvered them into the bay.

"Hello, island," she said into the storm.

The wind died down in that moment. The sheet of rain that had just been soaking her was a clearly-visible wall of water moving along the Strait, and she could see a second hedge approaching from the west. In the space between the rain, she thought she could hear the island respond in kind.

It was easy to spot a Cabot girl. The town was small enough that the residents all knew each other on sight, but even a stranger would be able to tell Winnie, Reese, and May were related just by looking at them. It was their ears, large and stuck out from the side of their heads like cup handles. Women who cared more about vanity might arrange their hair to disguise or diminish the prominence, but the Cabot girls prided themselves on the shared trait.

Chloe Passoth loved the Cabot ears or, to be more honest, she loved one pair in particular. Cerys Cabot, Reese to those who knew her well, had perfectly smooth lobes that reminded her of little seashells. She couldn't resist leaning over and taking one into her mouth. Reese squirmed and tried to push her off, but the accompanying laughter only emboldened her attack. Reese squealed and kicked her legs under the blanket. The mattress, knocked askew by their afternoon activities, hit the nightstand and thumped it against the wall.

"Okay, okay, stop, stop," Reese laughed breathlessly. "We're going to knock something off."

Chloe retreated back to her side of the twin bed. Reese stretched one arm out to make sure her lamp, mug, and book were still securely on the nightstand. Chloe was on her stomach and pushed herself up on her elbows to look at Cerys. Beautiful, redheaded, impish and wild Cerys Cabot. Younger than someone she would've seen herself with. Their nine-year age gap wasn't as scandalous as it might have been; Chloe had already started her own business when Reese was still in high school. But Reese was in her thirties now, and Chloe was just over forty, and not many people would find that worthy of raising an eyebrow.

Of course there were other, far more scandalous things about their relationship that could get the town gossips working overtime.

The rain sharply came to an end, a sudden silence that made both of them turn toward the window. Reese and her sororal twin sister technically each had their own bedroom, but they'd long ago knocked down the wall between them. Even though the curtain was down and May wasn't home, Chloe couldn't help but feel someone was just on the other side waiting to catch them.

Reese pushed the blankets aside and crossed the room on tiptoe. Chloe took the opportunity to ogle the frilly panties she couldn't help but think of as knickers due to how old fashioned they looked. She loved the sight of Reese with her long legs fully on display, and the sleeveless undershirt revealing the spray of freckles that ran from shoulder to shoulder. She bent a knee on the window seat and leaned forward with the fingers of one hand splayed against the glass.

"Is the rain gone?" Chloe asked.

"Shit. Winnie's home."

Chloe moved out of instinct, half out of bed and reaching for her clothes even before Reese turned around. "Is she downstairs?"

"Not home-home." Reese turned away from the window to gather her clothes. "but Barty's boat is here. Unless she missed it, which doesn't sound like Winnie, she'll be here any minute."

"Right." She pulled on her socks and then began searching for her pants. "I thought she was going to be gone all day."

"She sort of was gone all day, sweetheart." Reese came back to the bed and helped Chloe find her clothes. "It's almost seven o'clock."

"Shit. Shit."

They rushed around the bedroom. Reese left the room and came back with Chloe's shoes and coat. Reese led the way into the hall, both moving like tenants evacuating after a fire alarm. Reese went down first to make sure the driveway was clear before she waved Chloe down. They hurried through the living room and Reese opened the door for her. The front yard couldn't be seen from the back driveway Winnie was certain to use.

Chloe paused at the door. "For the record, I hate doing this."

"I know, baby." She cupped Chloe's face and kissed her quickly. "I hate it, too. But you have to go. Hurry."

Chloe left the Cabot house and walked at a quick pace toward the street that ran along the front of their property. It was more like a glorified alley, with twin ruts where the garbage truck came once a week to empty their bins, and she was confident she could make it to the side street without being spotted. The rain started up again when she reached the end of the alley. She flipped up her hood and jogged to the corner where she could find shelter until the storm passed.

A bell jingled overhead as she entered the laundromat. The owner wasn't in his little office at the front, and Mrs. Hudkins was the only customer. The older woman was stationed in one of the lime green chairs at the other side of the long, narrow space reading a magazine in front of the machine tumbling her clothes. Chloe took a seat at the front of the store, right in front of the windows, and twisted so she could look outside. Soon enough the rain would slow to a trickle and she could go back to where she'd parked without getting soaked. She just had to be patient.

While she waited, she opened her purse and took out her ring. She slipped it onto her left hand, stared at it, and on a whim decided to call her husband to see if he wanted her to pick up dinner on the way home.

There had always been Cabot girls on Coventry Island. In 1861, the founders commemorated the town's birth with a placard that was still in place on a stone outside the Odd Fellows Hall. The second name engraved on the memorial was Vera Berdie Cabot. In the years that followed there were never fewer than two generations of the family living on the island at any given time. They'd seen their little town through the change of century and millennium both, through countless wars and tragedies, a constant presence even as the descendants of the town's original residents drifted away.

A century and a half later, there were three Cabot generations on the island. Grandma Mairwen and her partner, Eliza, lived in the big family home on the hill. It was just visible through the trees as Winnie drove off the boat. She always thought it was ugly, a boxy gray-blue Dutch Colonial with two windows on the upper floor that looked out to the west. As a girl, Winnie had sat in the attic window and squinted with her nose pressed against the glass to see if she could see all the way to the Pacific Ocean. Some days she thought she could, other days she knew she was just imagining things.

Winnie's mother Ashlyn was the middle generation on the island. She ran PNW Treasure Chest, an antique shop which played fast and loose with the definition of "antique." There were certainly items which qualified for the title - a wardrobe from the turn of the century, Persian rugs, a wrought iron pull string doorbell, and more jewelry than any of the girls could wear in their lifetimes, though they'd certainly tried. The shop was also stocked with more knickknacks than your average Goodwill. Kitschy artwork, goofy statues carved from wood or molded out of plastic, gaudy jewelry. Winnie loved these little oddities the best. She once saved her allowance to buy an entire troop of mice dressed in Revolutionary War garb.

Winnie and her sisters, the twins Cerys and Maeve, were the youngest Cabots. They lived together in a beautiful Victorian house near the center of town. Winnie pulled around the back and parked by the detached garage. The rain was still pouring, so she grabbed the things that needed to be refrigerated and hurried inside. The lights were on in the kitchen but the rest of the house was dark. Though allowances were made for modern conveniences, a washer and dryer wedged into an alcove next to the stairs and rewiring for the kitchen and electronic devices, it still had the same charm as when it was built a century earlier.

As she was taking off her hood, she was startled by footsteps on the stairs. She turned and saw Reese, dressed in pajama bottoms and a T-shirt. Her red hair was pulled back into a tail to expose the smooth line of her neck. She looked flush, but she smiled and put a hand on the newel to change direction into the kitchen.

"Welcome back, Win. What did you get?"

"What are you doing home?" she asked.

Reese stood on her toes to peer into the grocery bags without bothering to unload them. "May said she would cover the store. Slow day, plus the rain keeping everyone at home. Did you get anything good? I'm snacky."

"Help unpack and you'll see. I left the stuff for work out in the car. Anything else is fair game."

"Hazelnuts!"

"After you help unpack," Winnie emphasized.

Reese started taking items from the bags to transfer groceries to the cabinet.

"You owe May one of your days off."

"I know, I know," Reese said. "If you didn't remind me, she would've."

Winnie said, "You also need to call Chloe."

"Why?"

"The truck's doing that thing again. It started on the second try, and it didn't give me any trouble on the boat, but I want her to take another look at it."

"Sure," Reese said. "I'll call her tomorrow."

Winnie shut the fridge door. "So what have you been doing all day?"

"Listening to the rain, napping, reading. I walked around in my underwear just because I could. It's so lovely to have the entire house all to myself for once."

"You could always move out."

Reese said, "I'm already pretty much packed."

"Good riddance."

"I'll be out by Monday."

Winnie hugged Reese from behind and kissed the back of her neck. "I'm going to run upstairs and change into my jammies. Then we'll steal one of May's garbage DVDs and watch it in the sunroom."

"Get something from the nineties."

"I know just the thing. Go set up the player."

Reese went into the sunroom. The stairs were between the kitchen and the front room, flanked on one side by the dryer and a pantry on the other. Winnie headed up to the second floor. Her bedroom was to the right at the top of the stairs with Reese and May's rooms were across the landing. The wall had been knocked down when they first moved into the house; they'd shared a room since they were infants and saw no reason to stop just because they were adults.

Winnie changed into her comfortable pajamas and used the right-side door to enter May's side of the bedroom. She crouched next to the shelf with the DVDs and glanced toward the yellow curtain that provided the twins with a small bit of privacy. The curtain was open enough that she could see that the sheets and blankets of Reese's bed were all tangled. She had two pillows that she ordinarily stacked together, but currently they were side-by-side.

Each pillow had the distinct impression of a head. Winnie furrowed her brow and stood up, crossed into Reese's side of the room, and looked at the pillows from up close. There wasn't a lot of room on the bed for two people, but she knew a dedicated couple could make it work. She tilted her head and looked under the dust ruffle where a small black bottle of lube had fallen. It was next to the fancy, frilly panties that Reese bought on a trip to Seattle "just in case there's ever someone worth showing them to."

Reese shouted from downstairs, "I want to watch *Hudson Hawk!*"

"Okay," Winnie called. She turned her back on the mystery and went back to May's movie collection. She found the movie, tapped the case against her thigh, and left without giving a second thought to how Reese had apparently really spent her rainy afternoon. She was an adult, after all, and most likely had a very good reason for lying.

Still, it was very curious. If her sister found someone to share her bed with, why wouldn't she share that information? They shared everything else.

Winnie decided to stop being curious and took the movie downstairs. Answers could wait. For the moment, she had a rainy afternoon to while away with Bruce Willis, Andie MacDowell, and one of her favorite bad movies.

CHAPTER TWO

WHEN THE twins were twelve, a girl in their class decided to pick on Reese because of her red hair. She was pale, freckled, and had big ears, so naturally Monica Higgins and her goons decided that made her an easy target. There were also enough rumors about the Cabot family to build creative insults. Reese was so easy-going that she barely noticed when the teasing started behind her back. Monica whispered to her friends whenever Reese passed her in the hall. They passed notes and made fun of her hand-me-downs. May had a growth spurt so she couldn't fit into Winnie's clothes, so she was spared.

Reese finally became aware of the teasing one afternoon before winter break. She walked out onto the playground with her books hanging heavily from one shoulder. A Wet Floor sign had been moved into her path so she stepped around it... directly onto a patch of ice. She skidded and slipped for a moment before all her books went flying and she went down hard on her ass. She looked around, eyes brimming with tears of pain and confusion, and saw Monica's clique laughing from the bus area.

They weren't the only witnesses. Winnie was there to walk her sisters home and happened to see the entire thing, from the movement of the Wet Floor sign to the dramatic conclusion of the prank. She ran over to help Reese up as May materialized from within the building. She looked concerned as soon as she came through the doors, aware without knowing how that something had happened to Reese even before she got outside.

Winnie helped Reese up and made sure she was just bruised and not broken. Reese, blubbering and trying not to cry in public, wiped her face on the shoulder of Winnie's sweater and held tightly to her. May, a wave of brown hair hanging in front of her face, met Winnie's gaze. They shared an exchange without speaking before they both turned toward their sister's tormentor.

Monica laughed. "Look! You knock down a witch and her whole coven comes running."

Winnie kissed Reese's forehead and whispered for her to wait with her friends. Reese nodded and stepped into their protective huddle. Winnie and May advanced on Monica's little army of twerps.

"Uh oh, Monica," one of the girls sneered. "You made them mad."

"That's right," Winnie said. "Hey, May, you know what people call a witch they've pissed off?"

May dropped her bag. "Ribbit."

Winnie said, "Damn right."

They held their arms out and began speaking nonsense phrases. A few girls backed up in fear, and even Monica's smug grin faded as she tried to make sense of what was being babbled at her.

Winnie flapped her fingers in Monica's face and shouted, "Boo!" Monica yelped and jumped back a step. She tripped over her feet but managed to remain upright, but the damage had been done. Her pants were white, and it was quickly apparent just how frightened Monica was. Winnie stepped back with a satisfied smile as the dark stain spread across her lap. The other girls noticed their fearless leader had just wet her pants and hands were clapped against smiles they wanted to keep hidden.

Monica fled. Reese hurried back to her sisters and wrapped her arms around them both. Winnie later told them she was happy to get justice, but she felt bad about resorting to such immature lengths. She felt bad for the bully who would now be subjected to ridicule. But when she saw Reese's face, the tears starting to freeze on her cheeks, she knew she could live with what she'd done.

They walked to their mother's shop. She was behind the counter as always, glasses perched on the bend of her nose as she examined an item being offered to her. The bell was bumped by the door and rang out to announce their entrance, and she turned to greet them. Her smile faded when she saw Reese's red eyes. She put down the item and took off her glasses with the other hand as she stepped around the counter.

"What happened?"

"A bully was being mean to Reese," May said. "Me and Winnie got back at her."

"Winnie and I," Ashlyn corrected absent-mindedly as she crouched in front of Reese. "Got back at her *how*, exactly?"

Winnie explained what happened. Ashlyn's lips pressed together in a thin, disapproving line. As she listened, she wiped her thumbs over Reese's red cheeks. She pinched her earlobes, tugged at the collar of her coat, and made her fingertips dance like spider legs up under Reese's pigtails. By the time Winnie finished her recounting, Reese was giggling quietly.

"You scared her with magic? You called yourselves witches?"

Winnie and May both hung their heads.

Ashlyn took pity on them, a sucker for the pathetic display. "I suppose under the circumstances I can understand. But you should never reinforce their ignorance about what we are. They'll find reason enough to be afraid of us without you playing games like that. You're both going to apologize to that girl, and I'm going to use it as an excuse to tell her mother what provoked it. So hopefully everyone will learn a lesson." She kissed Reese's nose. "Do you want to work behind the counter with me?"

Reese sniffled, "Yes, ma'am."

"Winnie, take May home and help her with her homework."

"Yes, ma'am." Winnie took her sister's hand and led her out of the shop.

May waited until they were outside before they spoke. "Was it bad, what we did?"

"We were protecting our sister. Sometimes that makes bad things... not okay, but justifiable. To a degree. Do you understand?"

May sucked her bottom lip into her mouth. She thought for a moment before she shook her head. "Not really."

"It's okay. A lot of adults get it mixed up, too." She squeezed May's hand, then began swinging their arms. "What homework do you have today?"

Maeve Cabot finally decided her too-casual customer was going to ask for love potions. The young woman in the fur-lined parka had been hovering around the front of the Stormy Mouse for close to fifteen minutes. She tilted her head to read the spines of every book on the shelves. She had examined the candles and paused to smell a wide assortment of them before putting each one back where she'd found it. She brushed her fingers over the sleeves of blouses and carefully examined the incense display.

May watched it all with a practiced eye. The girl knew exactly what she wanted, but she was embarrassed to come right out and ask. So she was browsing, buying time to work up her courage but also hoping she would stumble over what she wanted without help. May watched her from the counter in the center of the store, an octagonal island where she could sort donations and do inventory without leaving the cash register unattended.

May was tall, slender, and earth tone compared to her shorter, curvier twin's summer coloring. She wore a brown blazer over a matching waistcoat, a yellow dress shirt with a matching tie, and a floor-length brown skirt. Her hair was thick and long and wavy that she over one shoulder. Reese kept her hair shoulder length and was constantly tucking it behind her ears, a nervous tic that Winnie was also guilty of. May liked to leave her hair long and loose so she could occasionally hide behind it. She wasn't necessarily shy, but she thought it made her look more mysterious.

She was currently going through a bag of clothing given to them by Ada Short, whose husband passed away a few months earlier. May was sorting them according to whether they were in good enough shape to put up for sale. Later on she would cleanse each item, removing the various lingering traces of the previous owner. The work was rote enough that she was easily able to track the young woman's movements at the same time.

The browsing girl was young, but not high school age. Closer to college. She was very pretty, the sort of girl no one would assume needs a love potion, but May knew anyone could fool themselves into believing they weren't desirable. This girl probably just needed a boost of self-esteem. A phial of scented perfume might work as a placebo, but the Stormy Mouse wasn't in the habit of selling snake oil.

"Can I help you find anything?" May asked the next time the girl drifted near the counter.

"No. I'm... I was just looking for... um..." She moved closer and lowered her voice. "I- I need something to forget."

May was intrigued. She stopped folding and turned to face the girl fully. "What are you trying to forget?"

"It's not for me. It's for someone else."

"Oh, then I'm afraid I can't help you. I can't sell you anything that you plan to use on a third party without their consent."

The girl rested her hands on the counter. She looked desperate. "Please, it's nothing bad. I swear. I'm not going to hurt anyone or anything like that. It's just that there's this guy. We have classes together. I really like him. As a friend. But he's taking it to this other level. He's obsessed with me. And before you say anything, it's not a creepy stalker thing. I know if I told him to leave me alone, he would. But I don't want him to just... leave. I want him to forget whatever is making him think he's in love with me. I want to stay friends but if I break his heart..."

May said, "I understand." Anti-love potions, then. She had done a few of those, but she still didn't believe it was the right choice. "You want to be kind."

"Exactly. Some of my friends told me about this place. They said you'd have what I need."

"I don't think we do. There are certain things I could try, things you could take back and use on this guy so his feelings get turned down a few degrees. But I'm not going to do that. The best way to deal with this is to talk with him. Tell him how you feel, respect his feelings, but be firm about your feelings, too. Talk it out."

The girl said, "So friend-zone him?"

May rolled her eyes. "I hate that word. Look, if he pulls the friend-zone card, you're better off losing him anyway. It means he saw any friendship he formed with you as a gateway to earning sex. Now, does he seem like the kind of guy who would think that way?"

She thought about it. "Not really. But who can tell, right?"

"True. But be honest with him. Either you get to keep your friend or you find out that he wasn't a real friend to begin with."

The girl sighed. "All right. I didn't really like the idea of drugging him or whatever anyway. This feels a lot less sketchy."

May smiled. "You and I agree about that much."

"Thanks anyway." The girl turned and walked down the aisle toward the door. Halfway there she stopped, walked back to one of the clothes racks, and pulled a blouse off the hanger. She examined it for a moment before she draped it over her arm and came back to the counter. "No sense in making it a wasted trip, right?"

"Absolutely." May smiled and checked the tag as she punched the price into the register. "I'll even give you the mainland discount."

As she made the change, her fingers twitched just enough to drop a dime and three pennies on the counter. The coins chimed against the formica with a nearly musical harmony. The girl chuckled politely as May smiled nervously. "Oops," she said, picking up the money and placing it in the girl's palm. "Sorry about that."

"We're all butterfingers sometimes, right?" She gathered the bag with her new blouse.

When the girl's back was turned to leave, May let the smile melt away from her face. She'd dropped the change because she'd felt something. A minor shift or vibration in the island's energy, barely perceptible but definitely there. Like animals sensing an earthquake moments before it struck. She waited until the store was empty again before she walked to the front window and peered outside. The street was glistening with a thin sheen of puddles leftover after the rain. Normally she loved moments like these, when the storm was past but the air was still crisp and full of moisture. But now she could feel something underneath it. Something threatening.

She resisted the urge to lock the shop, but only barely. Whatever was coming would come, or it wouldn't. There was no sense in wasting worry waiting for it to show up. She took a moment to center herself and steady her nerves before she went back to work. She didn't want her negative energies or her fear tainting the merchandise.

The rain started and stopped a few times for the rest of the afternoon, like someone twisting a faucet back and forth. Occasionally the sun managed to peek out through the clouds and made windows up and down the street shine like the buildings were covered in gold leaf. May watched the clouds from the front window when she wasn't busy with work and, when the skies looked like they would remain clear for a decent amount of time, she decided it was time to close.

She locked up, drew the shades, and walked her bicycle out through the loading door out back. She paused to draw up her skirt, which she tied into a knot against her left thigh. She put the bag of goodies in the basket and pushed away from the broken concrete of the curb.

The Stormy Mouse was on the main drag of town, really the only drag they had. It was home to their restaurants and shops and anything of tourist appeal. Winnie called it the stage dressing of their town, the part they set out while keeping their real town private. May biked past Jo's Restaurant and entered the "real" town; the library and post office, the grocery store, the laundromat. The roadside trees formed a tunnel for her as she biked through the neighborhood and continued up to the biggest house on the island where her grandmothers lived.

The big Dutch Colonial, as old as the plot of land on which it stood, was the same color as the sky. May left her bicycle by the fence in the white picket fence and carried her package up to the covered porch. She knocked as she opened the door and stepped inside.

"Grandy? Meemaw? It's Maeve."

"In here, little girl."

Mairwen (Meemaw) and Eliza (Grandy), her grandmothers, were right where they always seemed to be: planted in their recliners in the center of the living room. The chairs were linked by a long table of tchotchkes behind them. May always thought it made the room look like the bridge of the starship *Enterprise*, with the television as the view screen. At the moment the television was tuned to a game show where Wayne Brady was trying to entice a cowgirl into giving up a car for whatever was behind Door Number Two. The overall gloominess of the day seemed ten times greater inside the house; the overhead lights were off, as always, and the curtains were pulled shut. May turned on a lamp and set down her things.

Meemaw waved hello, but Grandy was too focused on the screen. "Take the money," Grandy said to the contestant under her breath. "You always take the money. Cheaper in the long run."

"I know." May bent down to kiss the top of Grandy's head. "Those taxes. Oof. How are my two favorite ladies doing today?"

Meemaw said, "Nowhere near decrepit enough for you to condescend us, young lady."

"I would never, Meemaw." She smiled and went to the desk. She took out the iPad and turned it on. She opened the app that provided a free daily crossword puzzle and handed the tablet to Grandy. She liked playing and she could navigate every puzzle once the app was open, but she didn't like doing it herself. A commercial came on and Grandy bowed her head to read the first clue.

Meemaw said, "Busy day?"

"Just enough busy. I let Reese go home early. Hopefully she'll do the same for me on a day when it's not raining so I can enjoy the sunshine."

"Hope so," Meemaw said.

Grandy turned her head and examined May's outfit. "You're dressed like a boy again."

May smiled. "It's called androgynous. I'm dressed like a woman wearing a suit. See?" She plucked the skirt and held it out like she was going to curtsey. "If I believed I was a man, I would've become a man. But I'm not. I just like the clothes."

Wayne Brady was back on TV and Grandy returned her attention to him. May smiled and stepped around the pile of books next to her chair with the grace of a ballet dancer.

"How about you, Meemaw? Want to criticize my clothes, too?"

"No. You look like a lovely young lady. Just as you'd have been a handsome man."

"Thank you, Meemaw. Come help me start your dinner."

She helped her grandmother up and followed her into the kitchen. A few years ago, Grandy had nearly burned the house down trying to cook dinner. May volunteered to lend a hand whenever she could because it gave her a chance to see her grandparents every day. She also felt it fed her maternal instinct, the urge to take care of someone, without all the actual responsibility of being a mother. She could clean up their messes and make sure they were fed and taken care of, then she could head home where she could worry about herself for a few hours. She was too selfish for the full-time job of caring for another person.

The wall between the living room and kitchen was decorated with framed photos Grandy had taken over the years. Family portraits, landscapes, pictures of their houses and documenting changes to the island since the late sixties when she first took up photography. The last picture in the row showed May and her sisters standing in front of their mother, Meemaw, and Grandy, all smiling brightly for the camera. The girls were wearing pajamas under their coats and looked exhausted but thrilled. All three of the older women looked to be bursting with pride.

May touched the image from two decades ago and turned on the kitchen light. "Did you enjoy the storm, Meemaw?"

"Oh, we did, very much so. We opened the windows upstairs and just lay in bed listening to it all. It was like we were your age again."

May smiled. "That's beautiful." She was standing at the stove with her back to her grandmother. "So... did you feel anything this afternoon? Maybe around four o'clock?"

Meemaw thought silently. "Nothing out of the ordinary. Why, what did you feel?"

"I'm not sure. I'm... it was a... rumble. Like under the skin of everything. It felt like something was coming, and whatever it is, it's not going to be good."

"A lot of things like that are coming," Meemaw said. She came up behind May and scratched her shoulder through the blazer. "Always have been."

May smiled and patted Meemaw's hand. "I know."

"Tell me how your sisters are doing. Is Reese still single?"

"As far as I know. Winnie, too."

Meemaw sighed and shook her head. "You know we're gonna live until we see you three girls married off, so if this is a ploy to make us live forever, you can cut it out right now."

"I'd love to settle down. Really. But the island, you know, kind of slim pickings."

"Tourists come here every day. Dozens of them. And that's on a bad day. You find yourself a nice lesbian, or a nice straight girl whose mind you can change..."

May rolled her eyes, but she smiled. "Okay. From now on, I'll prey more on my customers when they come into the shop. Would that make you happy?"

"Yes, dear, very much." She peered at the items May had set out on the counter. "Now, let's see what you chose for our dinner tonight."

CHAPTER THREE

MAY GOT home just as Winnie and Reese finished making dinner. They reported their afternoon of movie watching, and May took umbrage at their classification of her DVDs as "trashy movies." Every film she owned was an award-worthy masterpiece and she would stick by that even to her dying breath. Their dinner table was set in a small nook where they could sit surrounded by windows. If the porch light had been on, they could see the trees flanking the edge of their property. May took her customary seat in the center with Winnie to her left and Reese to her right. Winnie served them all and Reese poured the drinks. After playing caregiver to their grandparents, May liked the feeling of being pampered a little bit.

May waited until they were all seated before she asked, "Did you two feel anything odd this afternoon?"

Reese said, "I was napping."

"I was off the island for most of the day."

May shook her head. "No, this was after you got back. And Reese, you were awake." None of them had to ask how she knew those things were true; May always had an innate sense of what her sisters were feeling.

Reese thought for a moment. "Nothing I can remember."

Winnie said, "Me neither. What was it?"

"Hard to say." She twisted her lips in an expression of consternation. She flattened her hands on the counter and wrapped her left foot around her right ankle. "A warning, maybe. Since I'm the only one who felt it, I'll have to keep my eyes and mind open. How were your days?"

Reese said, "Delightfully uneventful. Winnie brought back some hazelnuts."

May's eyes sparkled. "DuChilly?"

"What kind of amateur do you think I am? Of course DuChilly."

"Hopefully you two saved me a handful."

Winnie said, "You'll have to find out after dinner."

"You're such a brat," May said.

"Most people say 'you're welcome,' but you've always been your own person."

May laughed and tucked into her meal.

After dinner May helped Winnie with the dishes while Reese went upstairs to take a bath. Winnie took a position in front of the sink, rinsing the dishes before passing them to May for drying. She listened to the bathroom door shutting but waited until the water stopped running before she spoke.

"So what do you know about the mystery person?"

"There's a mystery person?"

"Don't play coy with me, Maeve. Your sister slept with someone this afternoon. I caught them." May looked at her, skeptical. "Okay, I didn't actually catch them. But when I went up to choose the DVD from your collection, I saw~"

May said, "You snooped."

"~I happened to notice that both pillows in Reese's bed were dented."

"That's some damning evidence. Maybe she just took a nap or something."

Winnie said, "There was a bottle of lube and her fancy underwear was on the ground."

May lifted a shoulder and batted her eyelashes through the veil of her hair. "Arwyn, honey, don't you ever just want to seduce yourself?" she cooed.

Winnie shoved her sister. "Shut up. It was just a feeling, okay? I'm worried. If Reese likes someone so much she's going to bed with them, but she's not telling us, that means there's a reason to be ashamed or afraid. Like she's worried we won't approve."

May paused and traced edge of the plate with her fingertip. "It's not like last time," she said at last. "I would know."

Winnie looked sideways at her. "Are you sure? May, I just don't want it to be like last time."

"It can't be like the last time, because I'm not lusting after anyone right now." She carefully placed the plate in the drying rack, her movements so measured she might as well have flinched at the Winnie's words. "There's no one I'm even interested in. So whoever she's hiding, it's not because of me. And like I said... I would know if she was betraying me like that again."

"Okay." Winnie squeezed May's hand, leaving a soapy imprint of her fingers. "I'm sorry for bringing it up."

May nodded but kept her eyes on the sink. Winnie washed a few more dishes and May dutifully rinsed them, placing them in the rack to dry.

"Maybe it's a man."

"She knows how I feel about that. She wouldn't hide him. She would just give me a heads-up so I could prepare the house for the assault of male energy." She stood still and turned her eyes toward the ceiling. She tilted her head as if trying to pick up a distant sound. "I don't feel anything like that. If there had been a man here, I'd have felt it. Even Reese couldn't wipe that out by herself."

May shrugged. "Whoever it is, she'll tell us soon enough. Maybe it's just a fling and she doesn't want a whole production about the 'relationship'."

"Who would make a production about it?"

May flicked her towel at Winnie. "Arwyn Mavis Cabot would."

Winnie laughed and grabbed at the dish towel, engaging in a quick tug of war before letting May win. "Okay. I'll leave it alone for now. But if you see anything, I want details."

"I promise."

By the time May got upstairs, Reese was reading in bed. She was dressed in a long baseball shirt, her knees bent in front of her to create a platform to lay her book against. She glanced over as May passed by her open door. May waved and went into her bedroom. She left her light off because she loved the glow passing through the curtain from Reese's side. It cast an orange-yellow glow over everything and made her feel like she was encased in amber. People who knew about the sleeping arrangements thought it was odd, two adult sisters still basically sharing a room, but May could hardly imagine sleeping any other way.

She undressed, put on a T-shirt, and crawled under the covers. She listened to the room, felt the energies swirling around overhead.

There was definitely something there, and it had definitely been another woman. Something physical and raw. She envisioned it like a wavelength, a smooth line that rose and fell with a rhythmic pattern. Someone had been in this room with her sister, and their energies had combined more than once, their heartbeats syncing. May's shoulders rocked against the pillow as if she was listening to a symphony by reading the sheet music, following along entirely inside her own head. There were orgasms, intense pleasure, joy, happiness, contentment.

May shivered and opened her eyes. She had no idea why Reese would hide someone who made her so happy, but she must have her reasons.

"Reese?"

"Mm-hmm?"

She decided not to say anything. "Goodnight."

"Night, May."

She rolled onto her side and opened her nightstand. She withdrew the small dildo she kept there, biting her lip as she placed it under the blankets. She let it bump against her hip as she squirmed out of her underwear and repositioned herself. On her back, one knee bent and the other leg stretched out, she retrieved her sex toy and guided it between her legs. Her T-shirt was pushed up over her belly and she moved her other hand to tease the fine hairs around her belly button. She smiled; she had years of experience teasing herself and finding just the right spots. That spot sent a jolt from the depths of her stomach to the center of her sex.

She squirmed under her own assault with a low and keening moan, using the blunt end of the dildo to tap and tease as a lover might. She parted her lips and extended her tongue as if in response to being kissed. She could almost feel their arms around her, their weight on top of her, taste their breath in her mouth.

Her face was flush when she came, both legs extended now, her back arched as she caught her hand between her legs. She rolled onto her side, mouth agape against the pillow, and she laughed breathlessly as she curled her legs up toward her chest. She turned the toy around, its base still caught between her thighs, and wrapped her finger and thumb around the shaft. She grunted quietly as she stroked it, thinking about her grandmother's words. She didn't want to be a man. There were people for whom transitioning was right, but she wasn't one of them. She loved being a woman, she felt right as a woman, but she could be dapper and manly without actually having a penis.

Still, though... May chuckled as she stroked her fake cock. Sometimes it was fun to play.

Reese spoke softly from the other side of the curtain. "Goddess, May. They had to have felt that on the mainland."

May laughed and raked her hair out of her face. "Good. I hope they enjoyed it. Night, Reese."

"Night, sweetie."

May returned the toy to its spot in the desk. Instead of pulling her underwear back on, she stripped off her T-shirt. She wanted to be bare after an orgasm like that. She needed to feel the night air on her skin. She kicked the blankets away, spread her arms out to either side, and smiled as she drifted off to a dreamless sleep.

Winnie took care of locking up the house, turning out the lights and checking the windows. Upstairs, Reese had fallen asleep with the light on and a book open on her chest. Winnie gently removed the book and marked the place before putting it aside. Reese stirred in her sleep but didn't fully wake. Winnie smoothed down her sister's wild hair and bent down to kiss the barely-noticeable freckles on her forehead before she turned out the lights. She checked on May through the curtain, confirming she was sprawled across the mattress as if she'd been thrown at it from across the room. She moved inside and covered May with a blanket for modesty's sake.

Once her home and family were taken care of, she went into her bedroom. Her room was simple, a former attic space which had been refurbished for her. The roof cut one of her corners and shrank one side of the room to just a few inches high. She chose that cramped space for the altar, since it felt as if the entire room - and from there the house - opened up from that spot. She took off her clothes and traded them for a simple cotton shift. She placed a candle in the middle of the altar and said a silent prayer to bless it before she lit a match and touched it to the wick.

She knelt on a pillow in front of the candle and held her hands in her lap.

"Mother of all, we praise you. Blessings to you and to us. Thank you for your protection today. Thank you for the joy and pleasures you brought into the lives of Maeve and Cerys. Thank you for the continued health of our grandmothers, and our mother. Watch over our father, wherever he may be, whatever he may be facing, and keep him safe. Let him know that he is loved by his daughters. Mother of all, watch over the people of this island, which you have given to us as a home and for which we are forever grateful every day. Forgive us for the slights and pains we have caused to others. So mote it be."

Winnie let the candle burn as she went through her exercises. It was a simply routine of pushups, sit-ups, and stretches that nevertheless left her feeling breathless and limber. She let the candle burn through the workout and afterward she sat on the floor in front of it to read. The candle flickered for an hour and a half - thirty minutes for each resident in the house - before she leaned in and blew it out. The smoke swirled above the altar and she smiled.

"Thank you, mother. Blessed be."

She turned to get into bed and something hit her. It was a hard blow, almost physical, but she kept herself from crying out as she was thrown back a step. The floor under her feet reverberated like glass near a speaker, a steady throb that would have made her think earthquake if anything else in the room had been unsettled. But the jars on her nightstand were stationary and the curtains hung limp and lifeless. The energy faded almost as quickly as it struck, but the aftereffects would remain for hours.

Winnie moved to the window and pushed the curtains aside. The tourist part of town was dark, silenced for the evening until the first boats arrived in the morning. She could see lights from a few houses in the neighborhoods, porch lights burning into the night. She saw a few boats gathered in the cozy harbor like calves returning to the barn, and the last ferry of the night had just arrived at its dock. She ran her eyes over the slumbering silhouette of her town and shuddered, hugging herself against the gooseflesh that had risen on her arms

"What was that?" she whispered. She thought of the feeling May had reported and knew the two had to be connected, but how? And why were they affected so many hours apart?

She closed the windows and went back to the altar. She knelt, lit another candle, and folded her hands in front of her.

"Mother of all, we praise you," she whispered. "Blessings to you and to us..."

Lighting another candle meant she couldn't extinguish it for ninety minutes, but she wasn't concerned about that. She had a feeling she wasn't going to be sleeping much that night, if she slept at all.

The floor jerked slightly under her feet as the ship came to a stop, but the blonde woman swayed with the movement like a tree in an old-growth forest. Her hands were folded in front of her, the strap of a purse dangling from her fingers. The purse itself swung in front of her like a pendulum. She wore a black coat lined in crimson, buttoned at the waist but open at the collar to reveal a gray silk blouse underneath. She was the only passenger aboard and couldn't help but feel it was a private charter. It made her feel powerful.

Someone from the ship's crew came down and found her waiting. "You're free to disembark now," he said. "Sorry the ride was a little choppy. Storms, you know."

"I know. I'm from this part of the world."

"Oh. Well, okay then. If you need a ride, there's a payphone outside the ferry offices. There's a number for a cab service posted. Sonya usually doesn't like coming out this late, but if you ask nice~"

"Thank you," the visitor said. "I'll be fine."

He nodded and said, "Okay then. Enjoy the island."

She smiled at that without turning to look at him. "I intend to."

The woman left the ferry and stepped out onto the pavement. The rain may have passed but the scent lingered in the air. She felt the moisture on her face as she began walking. The smell of rain after a long drought was called petrichor, but she wasn't aware of a word that fit the smell of a place where rain is a constant companion. She'd spent too much time in dry places and the time had come to end her exile.

The wide main road of town was vacant at that time of night, no tourists buzzing around the sidewalks and no unfamiliar cars with out-of-state plates. She strolled down the middle of the empty road. Streetlamps on each corner cast just enough light to create shadows under awnings and turn recessed doorways into black pits. She approached a shop at random - PNW Treasure Chest was written on the door in scrolled letters - and cupped her hands against the rain-smeared glass.

Everything looked ancient through the glass, like actual treasures from a sunken ship. Everything on the other side looked murky and unfocused. Seashell frames, orcas carved from driftwood, countless paintings. "Treasure Chest" was a bit of a misnomer, but the tourists certainly seemed to eat it up. She moved farther up the street until she saw the Stormy Mouse. Her smile spread wide and she smoothed her hands over the collar of her coat as if she expected to be greeted at the door.

The store was set apart from the rest of the strip mall, a tiny isolated cabin with a narrow alley on either side. Its front door was flanked by two large windows that seemed to be filled with the same display as the last time she'd seen it. Summer on the island was cooler than in most places around the country, so she'd still been wearing a long-sleeve button down shirt. Maeve Cabot had been in a sweater that fell off her shoulders.

She remembered standing in the doorway of the shop, her bag in her hand. She remembered May looking up and doing that thing, that little shake of her head to get the center-parted hair out of her face. May had looked frozen in the headlights, expecting a scene, but she was only there to say goodbye. She hadn't even gotten to do that because, for some reason, Winnie had been there instead of at work. When Winnie saw who had just come inside, she stepped between May and the woman she considered to be their enemy.

"Get out of their store."

"Easy~"

"Out. Now."

She held her hands up in surrender and turned her back on the Cabot sisters. She glanced through the window and saw May watching after her. It was hard to read the emotion on her face. Relief, sadness, resignation... what might've happened if Winnie hadn't been there to interfere?

Now, in the dark, she stepped away from the window and continued walking into the heart of the town. She could smell the wet dirt and could almost feel the trees soaking up nutrients. It was as if every leaf was drawing in a deep and blissful breath.

She stopped when she reached the corner and turned as if her attention was being literally pulled toward the unassuming little house on the opposite end of the street. One window was lit with the flickering light of a candle. Winnie's room, if she remembered right.

"Hello, Arwyn," she whispered into the chilly air. "It's been a long time. You told me to stay away and I did... for a while... but this is my home, too. And if you girls want to fight for it, then bring it on."

A breeze blew in off the harbor and lifted her hair, the tail of her coat, and she smiled as the tree branches overhead swayed slightly. It was almost as if the island was reacting to her challenge. She turned away from the Cabot house and started walking toward the bed-and-breakfast she'd booked. She hadn't been idle in her time away. She'd been thinking about what she would do if given the opportunity.

Tomorrow she would get her chance.

Reese gasped for air, kicking with both feet until the blanket cascaded off the bed to pile on the floor. She rolled onto her side, grabbed at her throat with one hand, and reached for the glass of water on the nightstand with the other. Her mouth opened and closed like a fish thrown onto shore by a wave, her eyes wide with terror as she struggled for the breath that just wouldn't come.

The seizure ended as quickly as it began, air rushing into her lungs like a dam had burst. She gasped hoarsely and sat on her knees, hunched over, taking deep and ragged breaths of precious air. She swallowed and looked around the bedroom as if she could find the source, but she knew it hadn't been a physical attack. It had been a shot across the bow, a warning, a...

"No." Her voice was rough and raw as she realized what it meant. It was what May had felt that afternoon. She jumped off the mattress and ran from her bedroom, not caring that she was in panties and a baseball shirt. She stomped down the stairs, vaguely aware that Winnie's bedroom light was still on but not willing to slow down enough to call out to her. She felt her heart pounding so hard against her ribs that the bones ached.

She threw open the front door and ran out. The grass was cool and wet against the soles of her feet. She felt the blades tickling between her toes as she stood and looked up and down their street.

"Cerys?" Winnie was standing in the doorway behind her. "What is it?"

Reese said, "Jessica."

A storm crossed Winnie's face. She shook her head once, a firm denial. "No."

"I know, Arwyn. I can feel it."

Winnie said, "She wouldn't even think about coming back here."

"She's already here. Jessica Vaughn is on the island right now."

Winnie's voice was shaking with a mixture of fear and anger. "Come back inside. Right now. We'll get May and we'll all camp out in my room."

Reese reluctantly turned and walked back to the house. "That will work for tonight. But what about tomorrow?"

"Tomorrow we'll worry about tomorrow," Winnie promised. She put an arm around Reese and guided her back into the safety of the house. She looked out at the street one more time before she shut the door, twisted the lock, and turned off the porch light.

CHAPTER FOUR

WINNIE GENTLY woke May and let her put on a nightshirt before the three of them moved down the hall to Winnie's bedroom. She insisted the twins take her bed, reassuring them she was positive she wouldn't sleep at all that night. Reese slipped under the blankets with May and held her close, stroking her hair as Winnie settled into the armchair by the window. Winnie looked outside before tugging the curtains shut. She and Reese took turns describing their "events" to May so she would know that they'd all felt the same thing. None of them could say quite how they knew it meant Jessica was back, but once Reese put name to the feeling, they all knew it was true.

Reese said, "I'm so sorry, Maeve. This is all my fault."

Winnie said, "Shush. That's not important right now."

May cupped Reese's cheek, accepting her apology without a word.

"Let's just make it through tonight, okay? We'll talk more in the morning."

Reese also didn't expect to sleep, but she couldn't deny there were stretches of missing time throughout the night where she must have been dozing. She even dreamt a little, although it was the relatively lightweight dreaming that consisted almost entirely of reliving memories. She remembered the bright and shining days of summer not long after high school. Winnie was gone in those years, living in Seattle for a bit, so Reese and May were alone together for the first time in their entire lives. Movie nights, slumber parties spent acting like pre-teens, putting together their plan for what would eventually become the Stormy Mouse.

Jessica Vaughn had grown up on the island with them, but she was a year ahead of Winnie in school so their paths rarely crossed. The first time Reese remembered seeing her was at a parade celebrating the town's founding. She was wearing a bright blue jacket, her ash blonde hair falling onto her shoulders. Her tall frame was tilted to one side so she could crane her neck, watching for signs the parade was about the begin. Reese had been staring so long that when Jessica turned and caught her, looking away didn't seem like a possibility.

"Hello there," Jessica said.

"Hi..."

Jessica had smiled and turned away again. Reese remembered her ears burning in embarrassment, though she couldn't have said why she was embarrassed. It was a simple interaction with a stranger. But when Reese passed behind her, Jessica had turned and reached out. The backs of their hands brushed and Reese instinctively twisted her wrist in response. Their fingers linked together and she smiled nervously as Jessica squeezed.

"I'm Jessica," she said.

Reese was still swaying from the abrupt capture. "Uh. Cerys. Reese."

"Sir Reesreese?"

She blushed. "Cerys. But everyone just calls me Reese." She looked down at their linked fingers. By this point enough time had elapsed that they were basically just holding hands.

"Have you heard anything about when this is actually going to start?"

"Uh... no. Nope. Sorry."

Jessica freed Reese's hand. "Thanks anyway."

Reese nodded. She continued down the sidewalk, shaken by the encounter but unsure why. She looked back and saw Jessica watching her. Jessica smiled and winked before she turned away. Reese chuckled at her own discomfort as she turned the corner.

She woke with sun on her face. May was wrapped around her like a koala, all long arms and legs bending in a way that defied the limits of human anatomy. Winnie's armchair was empty, so Reese carefully extricated herself from her sister's clinging limbs without disturbing her. She bent down and kissed the arch of May's eyebrow, tucked the blankets higher around her shoulders, and then went in search of their absent older sister.

Winnie was in the kitchen. She had put on a shirt that was long enough to reach the curve of her hips, showing off her long legs. They weren't as long as May's, but they were better defined, more muscular. Reese, the shortest member of their clan, would love to have legs like May, but she would kill for Winnie's. She must have fallen asleep at some point as well, because the hair on one side of her head was pushed up and flattened like a cat's ear.

"Morning."

Winnie looked up from the breakfast she was preparing at the stove. It was three slices of gashouse eggs, and the smell of the spices mixed with the smell of toast made Reese's stomach grumble.

"How did you sleep?"

"Pitifully and without true rest." She placed her hands on the kitchen island, one on top of the other. "What are we going to do about Jessica?"

"I don't know. I tried to come up with a plan last night, but short of picking her up and physically hauling her off the island..."

Reese said, "I like that plan. What's wrong with that plan?"

"She has as much right to be here as we do. We technically had no right to kick her off last time." She put the toast on a plate and put it in front of Reese. She went back to the stove and started another three pieces. "I'm going to see Mama after breakfast. I'm going to see if she has any advice for how to deal with this. Are you and May going to be all right at the shop?"

May came down the stairs in time to hear the question. "We'll be fine." She passed behind Reese and squeezed her twin's shoulder. She settled on the stool next to her. "We settled that whole thing a long time ago. I'm not going to let Jessica come between us again. Let her try."

Reese hung her head and focused on the specks in her eggs. She'd once tried to make them like Winnie did, following the recipe exactly and keeping careful note of the cook times, but she couldn't ever get it just right. She suspected there was some kind of magic involved, or maybe it was just the knowledge that someone she loved had gone to the trouble of making it for her.

"How did you sleep?" Winnie asked May.

"No dreams. I think I slept straight through." She looked at her sisters. "I guess I'm the only one who can say that, huh?"

Reese shrugged. "We were pretty shaken up."

"Well, so was I. But I had you two watching over me. So... you know, I felt safe." Winnie put the second plate of gashouse eggs in front of May. "Thank you, Arwyn."

"You're welcome. Jessica may not even be back to cause problems. Let's not jump to any conclusions. If you decided to shut down the Mouse and stay home today, I think everyone would understand."

Reese and May said, "Not a chance," in stereo. Reese continued, "We're not going to cower from her. If she wants to try coming after us, we'll be ready."

"And she won't have any ammunition," May said. "Last time she used us against each other. She can't do that this time."

"Right," Winnie said. "The island shook us up last night so we'd be aware of her. She can't play her mind games if we're ready for them." She looked at the toast still on May's plate. "Eat. Reese, I want you and May to be together today, so I'll take the truck to Chloe's."

Reese was grateful for the mouthful of toast allowing her to nod instead of speaking. She didn't trust her voice to be steady when it came to Chloe Passoth, especially on the subject of Winnie spending time with her. Chloe was married, a fact that would supersede any reasons Reese might give in defense of their relationship.

Winnie finished her third set of eggs and finally sat down to eat. Reese finished eating first and kissed both her sisters on the cheek before she headed upstairs to get dressed for work. The cloud of Jessica's presence still lingered over her, but it seemed less terrifying in the bright light of day. They had seen her coming, and Jessica's preferred tactic was sneak attacks. All they had to do was show a united front and she'd be powerless.

Her relief was so great that she started humming as she went through her closet. She just had to find some time during the day to warn Chloe about Winnie's upcoming visit so she wouldn't be caught off-guard when the truck rolled into the garage.

PNW Treasure Chest opened promptly at six-thirty to take advantage of the first boat from the mainland. Coventry didn't get as much tourist traffic as some of the other islands in the Strait, so there was no wave of arrivals which could go ignored. Ashlyn Cabot maintained the rigid schedule by living in the rooms above the store. It wasn't a proper apartment, but she'd had a bathroom and kitchen installed to make it habitable and hadn't looked back since. Winnie knew her grandmothers privately called it "the shoebox." They couldn't understand how their daughter could be happy there after living in a stately house with enough rooms to get lost in.

Winnie understood. Some people couldn't tell the difference between cramped and cozy, between cluttered and lived-in. The shop and the apartments were the place her mother felt most comfortable because it was a space she had cultivated and brought to life piece by piece. Winnie thought that was why she felt comfortable there as well. She remembered hanging out in the shelves as a little girl, reading in the sun-washed window as the world passed by on the sidewalk outside.

The little bell over the door chimed like a bird as she came inside. Ashlyn was out of sight in the back, but she called, "Be out in a second, Winnie."

"Take your time." Winnie paused to examine one of the new arrivals: a cuckoo clock that looked handmade. It had to be fifty years old. The base was painted blue and white to create waves, and two orcas were leaping into the air on either side of the pale-yellow face. Winnie assumed it was meant to be the sun. The wood was a little chipped on the sides and the paint was faded, but it was beautiful to her. She knew some tourist from Toledo or Parma would grab it up as a kitschy piece of local color for the rest of their Rust Belt friends back home. She was tempted to buy it herself, but she knew it would live a better life somewhere else.

Ashlyn bustled out of the back room. She was just a hair above five feet tall, her chestnut hair piled on top of her head like a shaggy crown. She made her way through the labyrinth of aisles and craned her neck to see what had caught her daughter's attention.

"Fifty dollars. Too much?"

"Just high enough to keep the casuals away. Just low enough to make sure it goes home with the right person. It's the right price, Mama."

Ashlyn snaked an arm around Winnie's waist and pulled her in tight, bumping their hips together from the side instead of offering a proper hug.

"Jessica Vaughn is back."

"Ock," Ashlyn said in response, or something that sounded similar. She dropped her arm and walked to the roll-top desk that stood against the back wall. "What did she want?"

Winnie followed her like a duckling. "We're not sure. The girls and I all felt it yesterday. May got the first tremor, then me, and then Reese was hit the hardest."

"Well, that makes sense since it was her fault."

"Mama!"

Ashlyn held up her hands. "No judgment. I'm not saying she's bad, but... be honest. If she'd kept her pants on, the whole thing could have been avoided, right?"

Winnie said, "Reese didn't know what she was doing. If she'd known the whole story, then of course she would've... would've kept her pants on." She blushed a little. "Anyway. We're not going to assign blame. We just want to know what we should do about her."

"Nothing."

"Nothing?"

Ashlyn sighed as she lowered herself into a rolling chair. "The island told you she coming so you would know to keep your heads down. Don't go inviting trouble. Don't put yourself in her way. She's here for one of two reasons. One, something that doesn't involve you girls. So, keep your heads down, let her finish what she needs to finish, and she'll leave again. Two, she really is back to settle some score. Spoiling for a fight. So keep your heads down, don't turn yourselves into a target, and eventually she'll get sick of waiting and go home."

"That's your plan? To do nothing?"

Ashlyn held her hands out palm-up. "Easiest plan in the world, right?"

"Easy for you to say." She shrugged. "But I guess it's the best way to stay safe." She went to her mother and bent down to kiss her forehead. "Thank you, Mama."

"You're welcome. Tell your sisters to come in here sometime."

"You should go see them. I don't want to spoil the surprise, but I know May has been holding something for the store. She wants to give it to you in person."

Ashlyn beamed brightly. "I might have to head over during lunch."

Winnie petted the back of her mother's head and left the shop. She knew her mother's advice was probably the correct course of action. She knew that the best way to find trouble was to seek it out. But she remembered all too well what happened the last time Jessica was on the island. She couldn't just stand idly by as her sisters were circled by a vulture. The least she could do was arm up in the event something did happen.

May was impressed with how easily Reese pretended it was an ordinary day. She came back downstairs in her normal ratty jeans and a sweater that hung off her shoulder, showing off a black bra strap. If Winnie had still been there she would have pointed out the visible strap as a fashion faux-pas, to which Reese would have countered, "Women have to wear them but it's some kind of sin to let people *know* we're wearing them. I'm not changing out of my favorite sweater, so would you prefer I take off the bra?" May smiled just thinking about it, but it felt forced on her face.

They rode their bikes to work as they always did. May hung back so she could watch her sister, short red hair rippling in the breeze. How was she really feeling? What was going through her head? According to Winnie, whatever force warned them of Jessica's return hit Reese hardest of all. "Like an earthquake," she whispered over their breakfasts after Reese went to get dressed. She was watching the stairs to make sure Reese didn't come back down. "I thought for sure she was going to have a seizure."

She seemed fine now, even to May's practiced eye. Reese had never been able to hide anything from May. They knew each other far too well, better than they knew themselves, and everything about her screamed normal.

They unlocked the store and began preparing it for the day. Reese went into the back while May stayed out front for the customers. They started the shop as an offshoot of their mother's store. She acquired her stock from around the island and nearby towns on the mainland. Sometimes she left the store in their care while she climbed on a ferry and set out to "replenish their inventory." She haunted every kind of sale she could find - yard, consignment, estate - for treasures she could bring back to Coventry.

When the girls were little, they loved waiting at the dock so they could go through the new arrivals. They always got first pick. Ashlyn allowed them to use their allowance to buy a trinket, with a discount if they helped her unpack and shelve. Reese started taking care of the ledger when she was eight. She could be flighty and irresponsible, but the girl had a mind for facts. May was a natural saleswoman. Her rapport with the customers was legendary among the islanders. Their neighbors sometimes smiled sadly at the tourists they saw leaving with a large bag full of things they didn't really need.

The Stormy Mouse was more of a boutique than their mother's store. They sold the fixtures of a home: clothes, candles, bedding. It brought in a lot of newlywed couples putting their marriage homes together for the first time, and it gave them an opportunity to share a bit of magic with the new unions. There had once been a reason for the name, but it was lost to history. Reese insisted May came up with it, while May distinctly remembered the words being written down in Reese's handwriting on their list of possible names. Winnie denied any knowledge whatsoever about where it had come from.

The origin of the name didn't matter. The store had been dubbed Stormy Mouse and that is what it would remain, even if they couldn't explain why.

May went to the front window and turned the sign over to OPEN. It would likely be a while before their first customers wandered in, but she was fine with waiting. There was a small bench facing the window where she could people-watch, so she sat down and planted her feet on the edge. She wrapped her arms around her legs, cheek on her knee, and looked outside. The sound of Reese fiddling around behind the counter lulled her into a daydream. It was the familiar feel of the store, the aura they worked so hard to cultivate so their customers felt at home, and the comfort of her sister being nearby.

In the sanctuary of the store, with the security of Reese nearby, it was easy to forget the threat they were facing. The island was about sixty square miles, and the town only covered a small fraction of that. The population was about three thousand souls. Jessica was somewhere among them, somewhere in those sixty miles.

May had spent years trying not to think of Jessica. For her entire life, family had been her one constant. It was the same for Winnie and Reese. No matter what went wrong and no matter what obstacles they faced, they could always count on each other.

Except for when Jessica crashed into their lives. The joy of her arrival was quickly overshadowed by everything that came after. By the time she finally left the island, she had come dangerously close to succeeding in what May had always considered impossible: she'd almost destroyed their entire family. The bedrock on which she'd rested for her entire life, the thing she'd always been able to count on, was cracked.

Her family was vulnerable, and she was terrified that one day something would come along and finish the job Jessica had started.

She just prayed this wasn't that day.

CHAPTER FIVE

WINNIE LEFT the truck in front of the first open bay at Chloe Passoth's garage. She could see Chloe through the office window, talking on her cell phone. Chloe saw her as well and smiled, lifting her free hand in a combination of a wave and 'be with you in a second.' Winnie nodded and wandered into the waiting area. Music was playing from a computer somewhere. It was crystal clear and perfect, and Winnie hated it. Growing up, there had never been a radio station with a strong enough signal to reach Coventry. The music they heard was faint, scratchy, and hollow. It came to them like whispers pulled out of empty space. Even prerecorded music was heard on gramophones and scratchy record players at their mother's antique shop.

Still, the music was good enough that she bobbed her head along with it as she waited. Chloe came out of the office before the song ended, tucking the phone into the front pocket of her overalls.

"Hey, Winnie. Truck acting up again?"

"Yeah. Same old problems. Do you have time to look at it today?"

Chloe nodded. "I can take a look at it right now."

"Thank you." She followed Chloe outside. "It's getting to the point where I think it'll be more practical to scavenge it for parts."

"If it comes to that, I want first dibs."

"Deal."

Chloe popped the hood. "So how's everyone. Your grandmas?"

"They're good. Cerys and Maeve are good, too. Stormy Mouse is doing well."

"Good, good."

Winnie said, "And your husband? How's he doing these days?"

Chloe's face was hidden by the raised hood, which gave her voice a slight echo. "Fine. He'll probably be by Will & Winn later today."

Winnie almost thanked her 'for the warning,' but she didn't want to be rude. "I'll be watching for him. You don't need me here looking over your shoulder, right?"

"No, no, go on to work." She straightened and tapped the engine with her hand. "It's been pretty slow all morning, so I'm happy for the challenge. I'll give you a call when I know more."

Winnie said, "Okay. Be brutal about it. If we'd save money in the long run buying a new one, don't sugarcoat it."

"You have my word."

Winnie started to say something else, but Chloe was already focused on the engine. "I'll be back around eleven-thirty. Lunchtime. Will that be long enough to know whether it's salvageable?"

"Sure. Oh! Could you bring me some of that, uh, what is it... that spongy cakey thing you make that's so damn good? With the powder on top?"

"I'll bring you a big slice."

"Perfect."

Winnie turned away and walked to the sidewalk. Her bakery was just around the corner, but there was no rush. She had a fantastic staff who kept the gears turning when she wasn't there. Keisha unlocked the doors and got the machines warmed up, Linda and Terry started the first batch of goodies of the day. Usually she was there for the middle part of the day to help with the lunch rush and bless the ingredients, the fixtures, and whatever had been made while she was away. Items bought at her shop bolstered spirits and refreshed minds. It opened eyes that were inadvertently closed and revitalized souls that didn't realize they had fallen asleep.

She breezed through the front door of the Will & Winn Bakery. The name was May's idea: she was Winnie, and she used her will to make her goodies. Everyone else thought it was clever, but they weren't the ones who had to constantly answer questions about where "Will" was. She used the back of her hand to sweep the hair out of her face as she greeted the regulars who called out to her. The apron she tied around her waist had the shop's logo on one corner - a tree with bare branches spread wide. A heart was hanging from one branch, and a crescent moon hung from the other side.

Florence, the former high school basketball player who towered over most adult men, smiled at Winnie as she came around the counter.

"Hey, Missus Cabot. Saw your sisters the other day. How come you look more like May than her twin does?"

Winnie laughed; it was a common question. "It's called sororal twins, Flo. It means the same thing as fraternal twins, but it's feminine instead of masculine. So guess which one people use more?" She patted Florence on the arm as she passed. "It just means May and Reese don't have to look alike just because our family was blessed with them at the same time."

Florence said, "Gotcha."

"Either that or the real Reese was stolen by goblins and they left the wrong changeling in her crib." She bumped open the kitchen door with her butt and shrugged. "Both theories have support in the family."

Florence's laugh followed her into the kitchen, where her staff was busy preparing fresh goodies for the lunch crowd. She paused to pluck a chocolate kiss off the cooling sheet and popped it into her mouth. Clark, one of her bakers, scolded her with a playfully stern look. She responded by wrinkling her nose and flicking her fingers at him as she walked along the edge of the table. All the treats waiting to go out were lined up like place settings in a dollhouse.

Winnie stopped at the middle of the table. She brought her hands up and pressed them together in front of her. Her toes curled inside her shoes and she felt the energy drawn from the earth, rising up through the foundation of the building and into the soles of her feet. She murmured the words of power under her breath and felt energy tingling in her fingertips. Just a little bit, not enough to unduly influence anyone who wasn't open to the experience.

She started blessing food when she was a child, cooking for her mother and sisters. When her mother would be sad about her husband leaving or one of the twins had a bad day, she could simply prepare a meal and lighten their spirits. Laughter if Cerys had a bad test, relief if their mother was feeling alone and lonely, or calmness if Maeve was feeling rambunctious and overly full of energy.

As an adult, transitioning to a career of food preparation

seemed to be a foregone conclusion, but she didn't want to make full meals. Too many variables were involved with an important meal. But baked goods? People reached for cookies and cupcakes when they were in search of something specific, even if they didn't know what it was. To fill time, for comfort, to balance an emotion, or just to satisfy a craving. If she could imbue those snacks with a bit more meaning, then everybody won.

She wasn't creating anything with her casting; she was merely redirecting what was already there. It was like pressing her hand against a frozen window and letting the warmth from her palm melt the ice where she was touching. She found the energy that was already in the world and directed it to places where it could do the most good.

Winnie finished her work and let her hands drop. She swayed slightly on her feet but managed to remain upright without leaning on the table. She blinked slowly and smoothed her hands over the front of her apron. Florence was standing by the kitchen door and had obviously been there long enough to start waiting. Winnie smiled at her like someone coming out of a trance and raised her eyebrows questioningly, inviting her forward.

"I know you don't like us to interrupt your casting."

"I appreciate it. What's up?"

Florence gestured with her head. "Lucas is here."

Winnie resisted the urge to sigh at the news, but she did roll her eyes. "I'll go talk to him. Thanks for letting me know."

"Sure, boss."

Winnie made a quick stop in her office to grab the latest books before she went out. Lucas was sitting in the last booth with a glass of ice water. She tried not to think of him as greasy, but it was always the first thing that popped into her mind when she saw him. He had the kind of dirty blonde hair that never looked washed, and he wore it long enough to flop across his forehead and hang over the collar of his shirts. Some people thought he was easy-going, but Winnie thought that came from a lifetime of being the richest boy in the room. No one dared to tell him no.

Lucas smiled as she sat across from him. "Winnie! How have you been?"

"Just fine." She put the book on the table. "Will that be all? I have work to get to."

He pulled the book over in front of him. "Winnie, this is just business. I'm not some Ebenezer Scrooge here to nickel-and-dime you."

"I know. Sorry."

She tried to keep the frustration from her voice. He opened the book and she turned to look out the window. He was just checking on his investment, making sure she was still worth the risk of his continued philanthropy. It didn't make her happier to be under his thumb. He loaned her the money she needed to start the shop, and it was his continued help that kept her afloat. The rent, payroll, supplies, everything that kept a business up and running cost money. Lucas had money to spare, and he was willing to share it, but there was no sense in throwing his cash down a hole.

Winnie also knew that they'd had a good couple of months. She didn't have anything to worry about because he was sure to be pleased with what he found. It was just the principle of the thing. She didn't like having him sit in judgement of her. She didn't like that if he got bored with owning the shop he might just take his money elsewhere and leave her flailing. He didn't need a reason to destroy her dreams and, even with her savings, she didn't know if she could pull it off herself.

So she sat across from him silently. She answered his questions, of which there weren't many, and tried not to shift too much in her seat. Eventually he finished his examination and nodded as he closed the books.

"Everything seems great, Winnie." He twisted to scan the customers currently in the shop. "Busy, too."

"Well, this is the busy time," she said. "It gets a little slow between ferries..."

"Show me a business on this island that isn't a little slow between ferries," he said. "Really, Arwyn, it's fine. It's more than fine. It's beautiful."

She felt bad for being so annoyed with him before. She wanted to end their meeting on friendly terms to make up for it, so she said, "I saw your wife this morning."

He smiled. "Did you? What's she up to?"

"Trying to figure out what's wrong with my damn truck."

"If anyone can figure it out, it's gonna be Chloe."

"Here's hoping."

He slid to the end of the booth and stood up. He took his phone from his pocket, sweeping his thumb across the screen. "She really likes hanging out with that sister of yours. Reese, isn't it?"

"They hang out?" Winnie said. "I know they knew each other,

but I didn't think they actually spent much time together."

"Maybe she said it was May. Or maybe I misheard." He flashed her a smile and gestured at his phone. "I should let you get back to work. Great seeing you, Winnie."

She nodded. "You too."

She gathered the books and carried them back to the office. He wasn't a bad guy. A little self-absorbed and not her type, but she really shouldn't hold those things against him. She hoped Chloe and Reese really were friends. It would be nice to give Lucas a reason to like their family in case the bakery had a bad month.

Chapter Six

REESE LEANED against a box in the back room, arms crossed with her hands tucked under her elbows. She stared at the boxes lined up against the far wall. The front three boxes were candles from the mainland, and the other five were linens that had to be sorted before they could be put out for sale. It would take most of the day, but she couldn't bring herself to begin. She occasionally heard May singing in the main room. May sometimes sang out loud when she was feeling anxious. Knowing May was feeling anxious made Reese think about why she would feel that way, and then she was trapped in a loop about Jessica.

She couldn't believe the bitch came back to the island. She could tell Winnie and May were treating it like an inevitable thing, like they'd just been waiting for her to show her face again, but Reese had let her guard down. She believed Jessica was gone for good and the fight was over. She closed her eyes and worked her neck, rocking her head left and then right until she felt it pop. If she could go back to the parade where they met thirteen years earlier, she would have turned and ran before Jessica ever saw her. Maybe it wouldn't have changed anything. Maybe Jessica still would have found her, but at least if she'd tried to escape, she wouldn't feel like everything that came after was her fault.

Reese and May were seniors. Reese was working at the lunch counter connected to the pharmacy. Jessica came in just after Reese's shift started.

Tall and older and seemingly so sophisticated. She had graduated. She was an adult, but still young enough so she didn't feel the need to treat her as an authority. Jessica angled her body onto a stool as she pushed her sunglasses up into her hair.

"Hey, Parade Girl."

"Hi." She was too awestruck to say anything else.

Jessica folded her hands on the counter and narrowed her eyes. "You told me your name, but I forgot. Sir something. That's not right."

"Cerys."

"Right! Sir Reesreeese." She chuckled to herself and drummed her fingers. "I'm happy to see you again. I'm Jessica."

Reese said, "I remember."

"You're a Cabot, right?"

"How did you know?"

Jessica gestured at the side of her own head. "Ears."

Reese smiled bashfully and touched the shell of one ear as she looked away. "Oh. Yeah."

"Can I get a grasshopper milkshake?"

"Sure." She turned to the freezer to retrieve the mint chocolate chip ice cream. Once she was looking away from Jessica, it was easier to find the speech centers of her brain. "I think you maybe knew my sister better. Winnie? Arwyn?"

"Oh, yeah. I think we had a math class together or something, right?"

"I don't know." She started making the milkshake.

Jessica waited silently while Reese worked. When she turned around to pour it into a glass, she said, "Do you want a cherry?"

"Always. Can I have two?"

Reese glanced guiltily toward the kitchen door. "I'm not supposed to." She put the glass on the counter and placed a single cherry on top of the whipped cream.

"That's fine. I don't want you getting in trouble."

Reese hesitated, then took a second cherry and quickly held it out to Jessica. "Don't tell anyone."

Jessica beamed. She reached out and her fingers brushed Reese's as she took the treat. She put it in her mouth, holding it between her teeth as she plucked the stem. She was smiling when she closed her lips and chewed, never looking away from Reese. Reese had cherry juice on her fingers so she rubbed them on her apron, cheeks burning for some reason as she looked for something besides Jessica's face to focus on.

"You're cute."

"I'm what?"

"How old are you?"

"How old~ uh... I'm eighteen."

Jessica pushed out a puff of air. "A baby."

Reese's awkwardness was elbowed out of the way by annoyance. "Not that much younger than you, am I?"

"Whoa, I didn't mean anything by it." Jessica patted the air in a calming gesture. "I just meant that you're a bit too young for me to ask out."

"On a date?"

Jessica arched an eyebrow. "Do you date women?"

"I've dated. Uh, I'm... I've..." She reached up and touched the back of her neck. "I like women."

"Do you want to go out with me?"

Reese was sure her face was burning. She was the only member of her family blessed with freckles and she knew they were now glowing neon. She twisted the bow of her apron between her fingers and shrugged.

"I... yeah, sure."

Jessica laughed as she took out her phone. "Damn, I thought you were cute at the parade, but now that I see you all flustered, you're even cuter. Tell me your number so I can text you mine."

The door to the back room swung open, shocking Reese out of her memories. Her shoulders jumped and she inadvertently took a step away as if she was under attack. May looked toward the movement and then scanned the unopened boxes.

"You haven't even started. What have you been doing back here?"

"I've..."

May tilted her head to the side. "Letting her in your head again?"

"More like letting you in. Worrying about what's going to happen if this... if she..."

May let the door swing shut behind her and went to her sister. They folded into each other, arms squeezing tight, heads nestled comfortably on shoulders.

"We're not gonna let it happen again," May said quietly. "We're stronger now. Okay?"

"Yeah." She patted her sister's hip and stepped out of the embrace. "I'll get to work on unpacking all this stuff."

May said, "That can wait. I actually came in here to see if you wanted to slip away for an early lunch. I know we had a slow day yesterday because of the storm, but~"

Reese cut her off. "An early lunch sounds amazing. What were you thinking? Flickers?"

"Oh, steak-frites." She clapped her hands, then linked her fingers together. "We'll explain it to Winnie that we did it to stay open through the lunch rush."

"Works for me."

Reese retrieved her jacket as May locked the door and turned the sign to closed. Flickers was one block down and one street to the left, removed enough from the main drag to keep most of the tourists away unless the wind was right. Smoke rose from the kitchen and sometimes drifted over to the rows of souvenir shops and down to the ferry lanes, and visitors would flock toward it as if they were hypnotized. On those days, Flickers could be one of the most crowded places on the island.

They were lucky. The wind pushed the cooking smells toward the woods, so there were plenty of stools available at the counter. The design of the restaurant was also meant to discourage tourists. Instead of kitschy cute island displays - the orcas on the ceiling of Coventry Diner or the totem pole outside of Sunrise Burgers - Flickers kept things simple. Green and white tablecloths, white textured walls, and sconces enclosed in wrought-iron cages. It was cozy and quiet, like a chic upscale restaurant, but they served nice and greasy breakfasts alongside their salmon burgers.

The waitresses were gathered around the soda fountain. Their favorite, a high school student named Tamara, broke away from the cluster and took out two menus even though she knew they would be unnecessary.

"Hey, ladies." She placed two fingers on the counter, one pointed at each sister. "Steak-frites for May, medium well, and a salmon burger with fries for Reese."

May winked. "You know us well, kiddo."

She gave them each a glass of water and went into the kitchen to tell the cook. Reese folded her arms on the counter and looked at May. She tried to pick out any telltale signs of internal stress or conflict. She knew her sister better than anyone but she seemed to be at peace even with the dark cloud that had moved in the night before. She opened her mouth to say something, anything that might be encouraging, but the sound of the bell over the diner's door stopped her before she could get the words out. She glanced back just as the new arrival spoke.

"Well, well! Look who it is. My favorite hometown girls."

The stress Reese had just been looking for appeared on May's face like a fist being clenched. Her posture straightened. She twisted her fingers around her napkin and bowed her head ever so slightly, eyes closed, lips tight, and she took a long, measured breath. Reese, on the other hand, slipped off the stool and moved to stand between May and the newcomer.

"You should go, Jessica."

Jessica held out her hands to indicate the empty dining room. "There seems to be plenty of room for me here. And it's a public restaurant. My money spends as well as yours does."

Tamara came out of the kitchen and froze when she saw Jessica. Reese knew the girl was too young to remember the actual drama, but the story had been passed around as local gossip enough that she surely knew who was standing in front of her. She looked between her and the Cabot sisters, started to reach for a menu, but withdrew her hand before she could take one. She folded her fingers around her thumb and looked to the other waitresses for help. They had also stopped talking to watch the standoff. It was quiet enough that they could hear people talking in the parking lot of the bank. A car door slammed, an engine came to life.

"Table for one?" Jessica asked casually.

"Actually she's taking something to go," Reese said.

Jessica arched an eyebrow. "No, I don't think I am. I want to hang around a while. People-watch. It's been a while since I've been home."

Reese said, "That was your fault."

Jessica tilted her head to the side. "Oh, Cerys, no. No, I left town because you and your sisters are maniacs. But I decided... you know what? This is my home. This is where I grew up. It's one of the most beautiful places on the planet. And I'm not going to let three little assholes tell me I'm not welcome."

May kept her back to Jessica. "Reese, let's just go."

"No. This is our island."

"Not anymore." Jessica stepped forward. "Things are going to change around here, Cabot. That's why I came back. If you don't like that, *you're* more than welcome to leave this time."

May stood up, head angled so she wouldn't have to look at Jessica, and put a hand on Reese's shoulder. "We'll take our food to go."

"She's not going to run us out of a restaurant in our own town. This is our turf."

"I know. But pick your battles."

Reese balled her hands into fists. "Ribbit."

"No. No angry witches," May whispered low enough so that only Reese could hear her. "Cerys, come on. We'll get our food to go. We don't have to deal with her, not right now and not today." She stroked Reese's hair, fingers pressing gently against the back of her sister's skull. "Calm. Be calm. Don't let her turn you into something ugly and mean."

Reese's hands relaxed. She took a deep breath and let it out slowly, never taking her eyes off Jessica. "Tamara," she said, "can we get our order to go, please?"

"Sure thing." Tamara finally snagged a menu and stepped around Reese to approach Jessica. "We can get you set up right over here by the window. It's got the best view for people-watching."

Jessica let her gaze linger on May before she followed. "Thank you very much."

May and Reese returned to their stools. A few minutes later, Tamara returned with a pair of to-go boxes holding their lunches.

"Sorry about all that," Reese said quietly.

Tamara shook her head. "No, I know... I mean, it's... I understand."

May took their food and headed for the door. They had to pass by Jessica's table, and Reese tried to summon the spirit of a Secret Service agent. She positioned herself at May's shoulder with one hand in the small of her back to guide her to the door. May had just pushed it open when Jessica spoke up.

"Looking nice today, Maeve. Are you seeing anyone, or are you still a virgin?"

May's shoulders hunched as if she'd been slapped in the back of the neck. Reese froze on the threshold. She held her left hand out away from her body and spread her fingers. She gathered the righteous anger boiling in her chest and reddening her ears, felt it spiral down her arm, and waited until she could feel it burning her palm. She turned, brought her hand up, and closed her fingers in a crushing gesture.

She was very pleased to see the genuine fear in Jessica's eyes a moment before the ketchup bottle exploded. Tamara yelped and Jessica recoiled in the booth as if she had been shot. The bottle was plastic so there was no shrapnel to worry about, but the sudden explosion of red liquid gave the momentary impression of a grievous injury.

Reese dropped her hand. She looked at Tamara, who had one hand over her mouth. "Sorry. I-I'll pay for that."

"You're damn right you will," Jessica muttered.

May said, "Cerys, let's just *go.*"

Her sister sounded on the verge of tears, so Reese finally left the restaurant. May was striding across the parking lot at a fast clip, forcing Reese to trot after her. When they were side-by-side, she looked over and saw tears shining in May's eyes. She felt a physical pain at the sight.

"I'm sorry."

"It's not your fault."

Reese's cheeks burned. "This is all my fault."

May stopped dead in her tracks. "No, it's not. For heaven's sake, I wish everyone would just get that through their damn skulls. You were a victim, too, Reese. The way she treated you..." She stepped in front of Reese and leaned forward until their foreheads were touching. The takeout boxes were between them, and Reese reached up to cup both sides of May's head. "Too fa'roo."

Reese couldn't help but laugh at their twin language. "Too fa'roo, din."

May grinned and stepped away. Reese let her hands drop. They walked together away from the restaurant, away from Jessica. She was stuck on the final shot, the warning that she would pay for the ketchup explosion. Given how much damage the bitch had done last time, she couldn't help but worry about what she might be planning now that she was back on the island. Whatever it was, she knew she and her sisters could fight back against it. At least she hoped they could...

She slung one arm across May's waist and pulled her close.

CHAPTER SEVEN

JESSICA LOOKED down at her blouse as she came out of Flickers. She'd done her best to clean up the mess in the bathroom, but there was still a horrible smear of red across her chest, spattered on the bottom part of her shirt, and dark blotches on her jeans. She would have to go back to the bed-and-breakfast to change. She hated that she'd let Reese get the upper hand on her like that, hated that she'd lost the first round of their reunion. It started out well with her surprise arrival. The Cabots should have been completely off balance by seeing her unexpectedly just when they were about to eat. She could have put them on the defensive within hours of her arrival. Instead it seemed as if they had expected her. Now she had to start from scratch, and it pissed her off.

She was about to cross the street when she heard a man calling her name. She turned and watched Lucas Passoth jog from the parking lot next to the bank with one hand raised as if she was a cab he wanted to hail. When he got closer his gaze dropped to her clothes and the smile faded.

"Oh my God, what happened?"

"Ketchup." The wind blew her hair into her face and she used the opportunity to shift her expression to something more polite. "A little accident at Flickers. I was just on my way to change before our meeting."

He said, "Oh. Well, you don't have to worry about me judging you for that. I've made my share of messes at the dinner table. We can push the meeting back a little if you want."

She shook her head. "I'm just down the street. It's fine. I'm really looking forward to sitting down with you and hashing out this deal."

"I am too! I can't tell you how long I've been looking for a partner who sees the same potential in the island that I do. I think together we can really pull this place into the twenty-first century."

Jessica said, "We'll have to get it to the twentieth century first. But I think we can do it."

He laughed. "Excellent point, very good point, yes. I'll let you go get changed. See you this afternoon. Welcome back to the island!"

"Thank you."

She watched him hurry back to the parking lot, then turned to scan the rest of Main Street. Kitschy little shops and quaint mom-and-pop diners like the one she had just left were fine, and the tourists seemed to love them, but the island could be so much more. The people who actually lived there were just hosts for the hordes of faceless strangers who wandered onto their shores, boosting the economy with purchases of driftwood carvings and seascape paintings. It had been their lives for so long they didn't know anything else was possible.

Jessica knew. She had been off the island and lived in the big scary world for her entire adult life, and she knew what these people were sacrificing. Reliable internet, for one thing. And the tourists, whom they cherished so much, could be spending even more money on the island. She looked toward the water and envisioned a hotel sprawling next to the docks. And to the north, closer to the center of the island, she could see condominiums, summer homes, cottages. Getaways for the rich and famous.

The island was a blank slate. It was untouched and pristine, but it could be so much more. She could put some meat on its bones and truly bring it to life. She had Jacob on her side, and that meant the deal was as good as done. The Cabot women were the only obstacles to her goal.

If all went according to plan, that obstacle would be completely obliterated within the next couple of days. So she was content to let them have their minor, childish victory with the ketchup bottle. She was going to win their war and get the island as her reward.

After leaving the diner, May suggested going straight to Will &
Winn to confess what had happened. "Winnie'll want to know what
happened. We had a run-in with Jessica, and you used magic against
her. Even if we wait until tonight at dinner, it will feel like we're
keeping it from her." Reese wanted to disagree, but her entire
argument was that she would prefer to avoid Winnie for as long as
possible. She hated that she used magic in anger, and Winnie would
be livid. She would make a speech. There would be scolding. She
truly wasn't in the mood for that. But May was right and it was best
to suck it up and take the bullet.

They took their usual table at Will & Winn - near the kitchen
but far enough away from the counter that no one else would sit
there unless things got busy. Winnie saw them and, when she could
take a quick break, made her way over to sit across from them. She
could read their expressions well enough to know they had
something bad to confess, so she braced herself for the worse.

"I assume you had a run-in with Jessica."

Reese glanced at May, who stared at her folded hands on the
tabletop. "Yeah. I screwed up."

"She screwed up defending me," May said.

"Still. It was my screw-up. Maeve tried to get me to just walk
away, but..."

Winnie held up a hand. "I'm not looking to blame anyone. I
just want the facts. What happened?"

Reese took a breath and then laid out the entire encounter
from beginning to end, including why they were at the restaurant
instead of at work. When she finished, her first question was not
the one Reese would have expected.

"Do you think she was watching you?"

"What do you mean?" May asked.

"She just happened to show up at the same restaurant as you,
at an off-time? I happen to believe in coincidence, but that's just a
little too perfect. I think if you hadn't decided to take an early
lunch, she would have found a reason to visit Stormy Mouse. She
went looking for a fight." She looked at Reese with compassionate
criticism in her eyes. "You didn't have to give her one, though."

Reese nodded. "I know."

Winnie flattened her hands on the table. "It could have gone a
lot worse. She didn't give you any idea why she might have come
back after all this time?"

The twins shook their head, but May added, "She said the island was going to change. I'm not sure what she meant by that."

"Nothing good, probably." Winnie chewed her bottom lip as she considered it. "Reese, you shouldn't have lashed out with magic, but I honestly believe you were provoked. It wasn't entirely your fault. And you came right here to confess. So I'm not going to give you the speech."

"I appreciate that."

Winnie said, "We should probably tell Mom about this. I was hoping we could settle things without getting her involved, but we may have to."

Reese said, "And what, have Meemaw and Grandy join her so they can fight our battle for us?" She shook her head. "No, they've earned their rest. They granted us stewardship of the island. Jessica is a threat we have to take care of ourselves. And now just because she's a mess we created."

May leaned over the table and lowered her voice to a fake whisper. "Reese still blames herself for everything that happened."

"There's blame to go around," Winnie said, "but none of it would have happened without Jessica. She decided to put everything into motion."

"We didn't have to fall for it, though."

Winnie said, "There's nothing we can do about last time. This time we can be prepared. We can present a united front, we can *talk* to each other. If we leave everything out in the open, she won't have any ammunition to us. Agreed?" The twins nodded, and Winnie looked at Reese. "Okay."

"I agreed."

"No. I mean... okay, now you can tell us your secret."

Reese looked at May, who was also staring at her. "I... what?"

"Your girlfriend." May hunched one shoulder and leaned hard against Reese's side, smiling goofily. "Winnie and I know you're sleeping with someone."

"You've been careful, but you're not a superspy," Winnie said, offering a gentle smile. "You don't have to hide her. We just want you to be happy."

May said, "And we want to have a big family dinner where we can all judge her and make sure she's good enough for our Rears."

"Don't call me Rears," she mumbled, a blush rising in her cheeks. Winnie covered her mouth to cover her amusement, but May laughed out loud. "You're crowding me."

"Come on, Reese," Winnie said.

"She's... she's shy. She's not out yet. I think... I think I need to tell her you know about her before I betray her confidence."

Winnie said, "I suppose that's fair. But are you happy with her?"

Reese couldn't help but smile at that. "Yeah, Win, I'm ecstatic with her."

Winnie stood up and leaned across the table to kiss Reese's cheek. "Good. That's the most important part." She pivoted and smacked her lips against May's cheek as well. "Troublemaker. I'll see you both at home."

She got out of the booth and went back to the kitchen. Reese put a hand on May's arm to keep her from getting up.

"Hey. Would you mind going back to work on your own?"

"Gonna go talk to your girlfriend?"

Reese ducked her chin. "I'm just... dealing with the fact you and Winnie know about her. How long have you known?"

"Just since yesterday. Winnie saw your room, and it was kind of a mess. Apparently you left some of your, uh, your stuff out and she saw that."

"Damn. We've been so careful, too. We just lost track of time yesterday."

May said, "Because Winnie was on the mainland while I was watching the shop by myself. Reese, if you'd just told me you wanted some time alone with your lady, I would have understood."

"I know. But like I said..."

"Yeah." May reached up and brushed her fingers through Reese's hair. "She's shy. But I like seeing you in a relationship. You get goofy and fly-y around girls you like. I hate to think I've missed some of that." She kissed Reese on the cheek. "Go on. I can handle the store by myself."

Reese said, "But that's two days in a row I've left you hanging."

"Special circumstances."

"Still. I'm taking a Saturday shift."

"By *yourself?* That's suicide! Tell you what, there's a movie I want to see, but it's only playing at the theater in Ramapo. You take Monday, and I'll spend the afternoon on the mainland."

Reese said, "That's a deal." They got out of the booth. "And I won't be gone the whole afternoon. I just have to go... have a talk."

"Take your time."

Outside, the day was still chilly from yesterday's rainstorm. May put on her jacket and flipped her hair out over the collar as Reese headed down the street. As she disappeared around the corner, May briefly considered following her but decided that would violate the mystery woman's privacy in a way she wasn't comfortable with. She would find out who Reese was sleeping with when both parties were ready and not a moment sooner.

CHAPTER EIGHT

REESE WAITED until she was out of May's sight before she allowed herself to panic. Even then she was careful not to let the anxiety flood through her. May had always been able to "feel" what Reese was going through, good or bad or indifferent, and she didn't want her sister to pick up any warning signs. She stepped off the sidewalk into the recessed doorway of a boutique, her back against the driftwood sign, and stared at the large plaster seashell hanging next to the entrance.

Winnie and May knew. They might not have known the specifics, but they knew enough. It was like seeing a grenade in the middle of the kitchen with no time to put the pin back in. They knew and the topic had been breached, so eventually they would demand to know who the mystery woman was. The secret was always bound to come out - it was a tiny island - but for it to happen the same day Jessica showed up was just monumentally bad timing.

Reese pushed her hands into her hair and closed her eyes. She should have just walked away all those months ago. She should have been smarter. It started in the parking lot of McGregor's, the only grocery store on the island.

They had no bread in the house, a minor emergency that didn't necessitate a boat ride to the mainland, so Reese ran over after work to pick up a loaf. She walked past the gravel parking lot behind the building and spotted Chloe sitting on the ground, knees up, hands in her hair. A broken paper bag was lying at her feet, with all of her groceries scattered out around it. Chloe wasn't crying, wasn't raging, she was simply sitting on the ground staring at the mess.

Reese cautiously approached. "Chloe? From the garage, right?"

Chloe just stared.

"You need a hand?"

"What's the point?" Chloe pulled her hands forward to cover her face and rubbed hard. "What's the goddamn point?"

Reese approached her like she was a stray cat, liable to dart off into traffic. "Well, to start with, your groceries won't be on the ground." She crouched in front of Chloe. "Or we could leave the groceries there and worry about what's going on with you."

Chloe scoffed. "You got a couple hours free?"

"Sure. Okay."

"Right."

"It's a small town. It's not like I have tickets to the symphony." She held out her hand. "I'm Cerys, by the way."

Chloe looked at the offered hand. "I know who you are. You go by Reese."

"Right."

She helped Chloe stand, then gathered the groceries for her. Nothing was broken, but the fruit looked a little bruised. Everything was probably still good, however, so there was no point letting it go to waste. They went to Chloe's car where they sat and talked for close to forty-five minutes about everything Chloe was going through. The water heater was failing. The roof was leaking. The back fence was threatening to fall over, and they were in a feud with their neighbors about who was responsible for fixing it. She was going to have to fire someone at the garage because he wasn't good at the job, but he was so nice that she dreaded pulling the trigger.

"And my husband is cheating on me," she finished.

Reese winced. "Ouch. That's bad enough on its own. Did he admit it?"

"Do they ever admit it? No. I noticed the way he became super protective of his phone and his laptop around the same time he started visiting the mainland a lot. And of course, those long trips meant he was never in the mood." She took a deep, shaky breath and closed her eyes. "I've never actually said it out loud. My husband is fucking someone else. I think I've seen a picture of her. She's not younger than me. Maybe more feminine than, you know, a mechanic. Not as familiar or boring."

"I'm so sorry you're having all this piled on you." Reese looked out the side window. The parking lot faced an alley, and there weren't any pedestrians on the main road at that moment. "You probably know what everyone says about me and my sisters. Our..."

"You're witches."

"We try not to use that word."

"Oh. Sorry."

Reese said, "It's not offensive. It's actually accurate, but when someone else says it, the word gets all kinds of bad connotations. We just prefer not throwing it around if we can help it. But yes, we can manipulate energies and magics. I think I can help you with some of this stress, if you wanted."

Chloe said, "What would it... I mean, do I have to cut my finger and squeeze blood onto a parchment or something?"

"This is why we don't want people to call us witches. You just have to sit there and accept that it's happening. It won't hurt any more than a massage, and I don't actually have to touch you."

"Sounds good to me. Better than medicating, anyway."

Reese shifted in the seat to face sideways. "Turn toward me." Chloe did as she was told, bringing her leg up into the seat with her back to the door. Reese brought her hands up. "Close your eyes and relax. Focus on the anxiety and stress." She cupped her hands on either side of Chloe's face, fingers spread. She watched Chloe carefully. "It's all part of a cloud within you, all the good and bad mixed together. Let me focus on taking out the bad."

"How can you do that?"

"I'm pretty talented with my hands."

Chloe smiled. "I bet you say that to all the boys."

"And some of the girls. Especially the girls. Now shh." She closed her eyes as well. She could feel the energy better than she could see it. She moved her fingers like she was plucking the strings of a large harp. "Sometimes bad feelings can be helpful. Sometimes they can guide us. But when they start to get so strong they blind us, we need to clean the slate a little. That's all I'm doing. I want you to see it in the center of your head. Push it together into a little ball. Squeeze it tight."

A wrinkle appeared between Chloe's eyebrows. "I don't know if I can."

"I'll help you, sweetie," Reese said softly. "Just visualize it, okay?"

"I can see it."

Reese pulled back and felt the energy spreading like a sunset, darkness rising from Chloe's spirit and swirling through the car. She closed her fingers and brought her cupped hands together. She turned and pushed it forward, out the windshield, and opened her eyes so she could "see" it dissipate.

Chloe opened her eyes. "God. What did... did you hypnotize me?"

"If you want to think that, sure. A lot of the stuff I just did and said was for your benefit. So it would be easier for you to understand what was happening."

"Well, whatever it was, I feel better than I have in ages. Thank you, Cerys."

"Reese."

Chloe said, "Okay. Can I give you a ride home?"

"Sure. If you need to be cleaned out again, just give me a call and I'll be happy to do it again."

"I'll keep that in mind. And... if I just want to talk again?"

Reese shrugged. "Still give me a call."

"I think I'll do that." She put her hand on Reese's knee. "And I really mean what I said. Thank you. I went from completely overwhelmed to... to renewed."

Chloe drove her home that afternoon and they exchanged phone numbers. A few days later, Chloe called to ask if Reese wanted to meet for coffee. Reese didn't like coffee but agreed to go for a walk. They found a walking trail in the woods outside of town where no one would overhear Chloe's relationship woes. Their second meeting and already they were keeping secrets and making clandestine plans. Reese told her sisters she was going for a walk, but not who it was with. More walks followed and, after a few weeks of meeting to talk, Chloe made a move.

"Are you gay?"

"I'm bisexual."

Chloe nodded, eyes on the ground and hands in the pockets of her coat. "My sex life is pretty much over. I tried coming onto him yesterday, but he just asked for some space. I go to bed naked, or I put his hand under my nightshirt so he can feel I'm not wearing panties, and he just gives me a look of pity that makes me feel rotten. I'm guilty about being horny. What's fair about that?"

Reese was extraordinarily uncomfortable with the bluntness of her talk, but kept her eyes on the ground. "I can't imagine what that would be like."

"I've decided that I'm being stupid. He gets to keep having sex. So why should his cheating mean I have to be chaste? I want to get fucked, I want to hold someone again."

Reese scratched the back of her neck under the collar. "I-I guess that's fair, Chloe..."

"Am I making you uncomfortable?"

"A little."

Chloe moved to stand in front of her, blocking her way. "I'm sorry. I'm only talking like this because I want it to be with you, Reese. I want to be with you. You've done so much to help me out these past few weeks. I honestly don't know where I'd be without your help. And I think I'm falling for you. You're beautiful and kind. You're everything I hoped Lucas would be when we got married. And the past few times we've met up, it's all I can do not to grab your face and kiss you."

"You're married."

"Technically. He hasn't been married for a long time, so why should I keep up the pretense?" She looked away from Reese and squinted through the trees. They could see the water from this point, and they could hear the quiet sounds of town filtering over the gentle roll of land. "If you don't want that, I understand. But just tell me to back off and I will. We can stay friends. I need you in my life even if it's just as friends. I just had to get all that off my chest so you'd know."

Reese stepped closer. "Can I kiss you?"

Chloe snapped her head around and said, "Yes, please, Cerys." Reese cupped her face and softly kissed her. Chloe kept her lips against Reese's as she muttered, "Oh, god." She grabbed the lapels of Reese's jacket, her entire body rigid as she leaned forward, her weight resting against Reese's. Reese parted her lips and explored cautiously with her tongue. Chloe's shoulders jerked at the first touch but then she responded with unexpected enthusiasm.

When the kiss ended, Chloe tightened her grip on Reese's jacket and pressed their foreheads together. "Oh, no," Chloe said. "Oh, no, no."

"What's wrong?"

"I just lied. I don't think I'd be okay with staying as just friends. Unless you occasionally make out with your friends."

Reese chuckled and stroked Chloe's cheek with her thumb. "Chloe, I don't think just friends was ever really on the table."

"Oh, good."

They kissed again and this time Reese began pulling at Chloe's jacket. It was on the ground moments later, joined by Reese's. The rest of their clothes followed quickly, and Reese kicked them into a sloppy nest that they could fall down onto. Evergreen needles still found them, poking pale and sensitive flesh at inopportune moments as they tried to shit their weight off rocks and pine cones. Chloe came the first time perched above Reese's naked body, one hand on the back of Reese's head and the other on her breast.

She collapsed, kissing the sweaty skin above Reese's collarbone. Reese toyed with Chloe's hair, aware of what a huge mistake they'd just made but unwilling to make herself care. Chloe was beautiful and fun and sad, and if what they'd just done took away some of that sadness, she was glad to be part of it. She was a bit concerned about other hikers coming down the trail, but at the moment she lacked the energy to move.

"Reese, did... what just happened... did you use any magic to make it better...?"

"No."

"Oh. Oh, wow. So... it's just... like that?"

Reese laughed. "When you're with the right person, yeah." She realized what she said. "Not that I'm implying I'm..."

"Sh," Chloe said. "I know what you meant."

"Okay." She kissed Chloe's hair.

"I want to make you feel that good. Teach me how I can do that."

Reese said, "You bet."

They'd eventually gotten up, gotten dressed, and continued on their hike as if nothing happened. But later that day, before her shower, Reese had shaken a veritable forest out of her pants and shoes which proved it was real. She opened her eyes and looked at the plaster seashell. Winnie would be furious with her. Adultery was a huge sin in the Cabot family. For most of her life she'd assumed it was the one thing all three of them considered unforgiveable.

Now all she could do was hope she'd always been wrong.

CHAPTER NINE

CHLOE USHERED Reese into her office and shut the door as soon as she arrived at the garage. She needed to finish with a customer, so Reese took a seat at the desk and tried to wait patiently. Secrecy had always been the backbone of their relationship. Lucas couldn't find out because he would go ballistic. Winnie couldn't find out because adultery made her furious. Their father cheated on their mother, a betrayal none of them had ever really gotten over. If Winnie knew Reese grew up to be the other woman...

The door opened and Chloe came into the office. "What's wrong?"

"Winnie and May know I'm seeing someone. It's only a matter of time before they figure out it's you." She linked her fingers together and twisted her thumbs. "I don't know what to do."

Chloe took a seat on the customer-side of the desk. "Oh. I was hoping it was something about the truck repairs." She stared out the window. "Is there a chance Winnie will understand?"

Reese shook her head. "She loves our father, but she throws away any birthday cards or emails he sends her without even opening them. She cut him out of her life like he was a cancer. Explanations don't matter. Reasons don't matter. Cheaters are the scum of the earth, in her opinion."

"I kind of always agreed with her, to be honest," Chloe said.

"You weren't angry at your dad for what he did?"

"Sure."

"So…"

Reese shrugged. "I liked you too much to really care."

Chloe stood and went around the desk. She turned Reese's chair, knelt in front of her, and kissed her. Reese put her hands on Chloe's shoulders and returned the kiss. They kept it brief just in case any of Chloe's employees wandered back.

"I would give up so much if I could go back in time and meet you first. Do you have any magic spells like that?"

"Sorry, sweetie." She touched Chloe's hair, dropping her hand to brush her fingers over the curve of her cheek. "Sometimes I feel guilty that you had to go through so much shit just so we could meet."

"Don't. Meeting you made all the shit worth it."

Reese blinked away the moisture in her eyes. "I love you, Chloe."

"Even if it costs you your sisters?"

A tear broke free, but Reese nodded. "I don't know what I'd do without them. But I don't even want to think about life without you."

Chloe leaned in again, hugging Reese tightly. "I love you, too."

Reese pressed her face against Chloe's collar and breathed deeply. She smelled like grease and sweat, firing Reese's arousal. She pushed her away before the feeling could get too powerful.

"I'll talk to them tonight. Test the waters."

"Okay. Call me afterward if you need to talk."

Reese teased the lapel of Chloe's overalls. "What if I call you just to listen to you breathe on the other end of the line while I fall asleep."

Chloe rolled her eyes back. "Oh, such a romantic." She kissed Reese again and whispered, "I love you," one more time before stepping away from her. "It's going to work out. You'll see."

"I hope so."

She wanted to be hopeful, but she couldn't help thinking about the awful timing. For the truth to come out on the same day Jessica returned to the island wasn't just getting wedged between a rock and a hard place. It was being shot at from all directions with nothing to take cover behind.

She just hoped she had enough time to avoid the bullets now

that she'd seen them coming.

Jessica had forgotten how the island smelled, how the breeze coming off the water gave a chill to even the warmest days. Everywhere else she'd been in the world felt stifling and too hot by comparison. She spent her morning touring the place she once called home. She hadn't been born there, but her parents moved to Coventry when she was in the second grade. It was the closest to a hometown she'd ever had until the Cabot girls decided they had more of a claim to it.

It only took her about an hour to walk the perimeter of the island, so she had plenty of time to meander down side streets. There were some new houses, a few storefronts with different signage, but for the most part it was as if the town was preserved in amber. She appreciated that some people didn't like change, but that was unfair to everyone else living there. Didn't the teenagers deserve to be part of the larger world?

Her plans would change the island, yes. But it would be a change for the better. It would be transformative and evolutionary. It was the opposite of their current stagnation, and anyone who stood in the way would either see the error of their ways or be left behind.

She'd spent the last few years living in Seattle, first for college and then working for GreenVault Development Company. She had overseen a few local projects to earn her stripes. She spearheaded a revitalization project of a block in Hilltop which helped her catch the eye of the company CEO. She used the opportunity to mention Coventry and the potential goldmine it presented. He gave her the okay to put out feelers, and that was when she met Lucas Passoth. He had the money and the vision required for her plan. By the end of their first conversation, he was not only onboard but she'd convinced him it was all his idea. Now they just had to get the development plans past the Chamber of Commerce.

And, of course, Arwyn Cabot and the twins. Lucas would help her with the Chamber, but the Cabots were all hers.

She didn't want to confront Winnie at work where she would no doubt be the most powerful. She needed to catch her off-guard and exposed like she'd done with Reese and May. She found a bench in front of the bank from which she could see the front and side door of Will & Winn. The smells drifting down the street were heavenly, but she refused to go inside and buy something. She didn't want to approach from a subservient position, encountering Winnie as a customer. They needed to be on even footing. But damn, it had gotten her mouth watering.

Winnie finally came outside, purse hooked over her shoulder as she buttoned her jacket. She started walking north and Jessica followed. The Cabot house was a few blocks away, and Jessica timed her approach to happen at the halfway point between work and home. She quickened her pace and caught up just before Winnie crossed the street.

"Just the woman I wanted to see," she said.

Winnie turned and her expression soured. "I don't have anything to say to you, Miss Vaughn."

"So formal! But I didn't expect you to carry the conversation, 'Miss Cabot.' In fact, you don't have to say a word." She moved her bag so that it was in front of her and reached inside for a manila envelope. "There's something so analog about printed photographs, but I didn't want to just show you my phone and then email copies to you." She held it out. "These are for you."

Winnie didn't even look down. "The last time you were here was supposed to be the last time you were *ever* here, Jessica. After what you did to my sisters—"

Jessica let some of her ire seep through. "Yes, the holy Cabot girls. How dare anyone taint their precious existence?" She withdrew the envelope. "You have a choice, Arwyn. The information in this envelope is a simple truth. It's not something I manipulated or created, it's just something I happened to get my hands on. It's something you will be better of knowing. But you can walk away right now and bury your head in the sand. You can live in ignorance and pretend I never showed up."

Winnie said, "I think I'll do that. Thanks." She turned to walk away.

"One of your sisters is keeping a huge secret from you, Winnie. Something you would consider a betrayal. She's keeping it from you because she knows it would change the way you look at her. Even if you don't know what it is, it's already affecting your bond. It's a breakwater between you. Whether you admit it or not, the block is there. If you know what it is, you can maybe work at fixing it."

There was a long pause where Winnie didn't turn around, but she also wasn't walking away anymore. Jessica let the moment stretch out.

"This isn't a scheme. This existed before I came back. It's

something you might have seen in the newspaper if this island had anything resembling real journalism."

Winnie finally turned around. "You're going to tell me who Cerys is sleeping with, aren't you? And whoever it is, it's going to break my heart."

"Like I said. I'm just providing the information."

She held the envelope out again, and this time Winnie took it. She managed not to smile as she put her hands in the pockets of her jacket and looked down at her shoes. Winnie opened the envelope and slid the papers out. It took all of Jessica's strength not to pump her fist or shout in victory. She remained calm and composed as Winnie shuffled though the photographs. She went slowly, looking at each one before moving to the next.

Jessica knew the exact order of the pictures: Reese walking out of Chloe Passoth's garage, head turned to check for traffic as she crossed the street. Chloe and Reese sitting in Chloe's car outside Flickers, Reese turned sideways in the seat with her arm extended toward Chloe's lap. Chloe on the porch of the Cabot house, shirt untucked and shoes hanging from her fingertips as she went down the steps. Reese and Chloe coming out of a hotel in Shield, a building Winnie surely recognized from her many trips to the mainland.

"What... what is this?" Winnie said.

Jessica reveled in how weak her voice was. "That's the married woman your sister is fucking."

"Goddess damn you." There were tears in Winnie's voice now. Jessica wanted to laugh. All the years she'd spent thinking about home but knowing the goddamn witches would just run her out again. Coming home only to have Reese humiliate her with the ketchup stunt. It felt great to hear the powerful older sister crack like this.

"Don't blame me, Winnie. I didn't throw them in bed together. They made that decision on their own. I started snooping around for skeletons in your family's closet, and a little bird dropped this in my lap. I never thought I'd find something so sweet, but I don't look gift horses in the mouth. For the time being, Lucas doesn't know these pictures exist. He doesn't have to ever know about them."

"Blackmail," Winnie said. "What? What is it?"

"You'll find out in due time. For now, enjoy the pictures. You can keep those. I have plenty of copies." She grinned. "It's been wonderful seeing you again, Winnie. And I can't begin to tell you how great it is to be home. I've really missed this place."

She turned around and walked away, victorious, leaving Winnie Cabot sniffling on the sidewalk behind her.

Chapter Ten

REESE FINISHED the day at Stormy Mouse, avoiding all of May's questioning looks and leading silences. Being a twin meant they had their own language but also meant they could hold entire conversations without saying a word. May pushed. Reese retreated. She couldn't bring herself to think about what she was going to say later, how she was going to approach it. Should she start with how much she and Chloe cared for each other, or was that emotionally manipulative? Did she explain how it happened so maybe they'd understand? Was there any way into the reveal which would overshadow the adultery and make it acceptable?

The day seemed to drag and rush endlessly onward at the same time until finally, and far before she was ready, it was time to go home. May suggested picking up takeout from the Lighthouse Café for dinner, and Reese agreed because it was one less thing to think about. It was all she could do to pedal her bike without crashing. May was concerned but also knew her sister well enough not to pry. May went to check on their grandmothers and Reese went straight home.

The house was quiet and still when she arrived. She left her takeout on the kitchen counter and took out her phone. She leaned against the fridge as she listened to the phone ring on the other end. Finally it went to voicemail.

"Winnie, it's me. I need you to come home as soon as you can.

I think we need to have a talk. It's not going to be fun, but I think it has to happen as soon as possible. So... whenever you get a chance to leave work, May is at Grandy and Meemaw's, so... uh... we already have takeout."

When she hung up, she leaned against the living room wall to watch the sun move across the carpet. She was still there when May came home. She was earlier than usual, implying she'd hurried through checking on their grandmothers so she could get home. She had just come through the front door when Reese heard someone moving around upstairs. Reese moved to the front hall, surprised to see Winnie coming down.

"You've been here this whole time?"

Winnie nodded. She stopped a few steps away from the bottom with her hand on the railing, looking down at Reese. The anger in her eyes and the set of her jaw punched through the center of Reese's chest like an icepick. When Reese spoke again, her voice was small.

"You know?"

May looked between her sisters. "Know what? Reese, what's going on? Winnie? Are you sick?"

"So it's true?" Winnie asked, ignoring May.

Reese didn't trust herself to speak, so she nodded. She kept her gaze locked on the bottom stair so she didn't have to see Winnie's expression. Her eyes were already tearing up.

Winnie came down to the floor and stood in front of Reese. Winnie was an inch taller than Reese but, at the moment, the height difference seemed to be measured in feet. Winnie seemed to tower over her cringing sister. May stood to one side, one hand almost touching her mouth, unsure what was unfolding in front of her but scared to look away.

"I'm sorry."

"Do you have any idea what you were doing?" Reese started to respond but Winnie kept speaking. "Did you even care? Did it even cross your mind that, beyond how *wrong* it was, it was also so very, very stupid?"

May clapped her hands together, making a sharp sound that made both of her sisters jump and look at her. "Someone tell me what's going on right now, please!" she wailed.

Winnie held out a rolled-up manila envelope and locked her gaze back on Reese. "That."

May took the envelope, unrolled it, and slipped out the

photos. She frowned as she examined each one carefully. Her cheeks became red when she realized what they were, and what they meant. She looked at Reese.

"Is this your girlfriend?" May asked. "She's pretty."

"That's Chloe Passoth," Winnie said. "Our mechanic. Wife of the man who keeps Will & Winn running, the man who owns a percentage of most businesses on this island."

May said, "Oh."

Reese said, "Winnie, I..."

"Shut up. I don't care what you have to say. I thought of it all upstairs. You're in love with her or you didn't mean for it to go this far, or you didn't set out to hurt anyone. I heard it all before, from Daddy. We all heard it back then. Or at least I thought we did. How could you do this, Reese? She's a married woman."

"He was cheating on her." Reese's voice was small and pathetic. She had shrunken in on herself, one arm across her chest to grip the opposite bicep.

Winnie said, "Well, that makes it all okay!"

"Maybe it does," May said. "I mean... I mean... i-if he was cheating on her, then maybe he won't care that she's sleeping with someone else, too."

"I know him," Winnie said. "I deal with him all the time. He's nice and he's friendly, but he's not a good man. If he knew his wife was sleeping with another woman, he would consider it an attack on his masculinity. He'd lash out. And you know who he would take it out on, Reese? Not you. No, he's too smart to just go after you. But maybe suddenly Will & Winn doesn't seem like such a good investment anymore. You know that I've always been terrified that the day will come that he'd just randomly decide to dump it. Well, thank you so much for giving him a reason!"

Her voice had risen several decibels, so May stepped closer. "Maybe we can all just calm down..."

"You can't be on her side," Winnie said. "You've been through all this before. Only this time, *I* was the one who got screwed because Cerys couldn't keep her damnable hands to herself!"

Reese shrunk away. May dropped her hands and looked at the floor.

"And the worst part of it all," Winnie said, "the worst part of this whole fucking thing is that I know exactly what I'm doing. Jessica Vaughn dropped this bombshell on me knowing exactly how I would respond. And it just makes me so livid that I feel like I'm supposed to give you a pass just because of where the information came from. Fuck that."

"Winnie, the language," May said. "Please, stop saying that word."

"You curse all the time."

"But you don't!" May shouted. "I hate hearing you say that word, so please, stop it!"

Winnie stepped closer to Reese, almost in her face now. "When you were with her, did you think about what you were doing? What you were inviting into our lives? The pain and the uncertainty? Did you even consider you might be handing someone like Jessica Vaughn exactly the ammunition she needed to drive a wedge between us?"

Reese finally managed to meet her sister's eye. "Yes. I did."

Winnie took a slow, deep breath and turned her back on Reese. "Get out."

"What?" May said.

"Get out of this house."

May stepped between them again. "You can't be serious. This is her home, too, Arwyn."

Winnie said, "This *was* her home. Just like it was Daddy's home until he betrayed his family. Reese committed adultery. She slept with the wife of a man who could destroy everything I've built on a whim. She just admitted she knew what she was doing and did it anyway. I don't want her in this house."

May started to argue, but Reese cut her off with a wave of her hand. "You know what, Maeve, don't bother. I don't want to be in this house, either."

"Don't you dare pretend you're the victim," Winnie said.

"All I did was fall in love."

Winnie turned. "All you did was fuck the wrong person. Again."

Reese grabbed her jacket. May started to go after her, stopped and looked at Winnie, and ended up hovering between the two with a plea dying on her lips before she could give voice to it. When Reese slammed open the back door, May's shoulders jerked and she flinched. She brought both hands up to the top of her head and sagged against the counter. Winnie sagged as if all the energy had just been drained from her body and she grabbed the newel post of the stairs.

"I'm going to bed. Please put my dinner in the fridge, Maeve."

"Arwyn, please..."

Winnie was already going back up the stairs. "Goodnight."

May realized she was still holding the pictures. She threw them, letting them scatter like a deck of cards on the hall floor in front of the washing machine. She backed up into the corner made by the lower cabinets and sank down, hands over her face as she sobbed.

Upstairs, Winnie went into her room and stared at the altar and the pillow in front of it with the imprint of her knees still visible from the night before. Her fingers twitched. Her brain and her power knew what was supposed to happen, but her body was unwilling. She walked over and picked up one of the candles, and wrapped her fingers around it. The prayer almost slipped out unbidden but she stopped it. If she did recite it, she wouldn't be able to put her heart behind a blessing for Reese. She would leave it out, and there would be no coming back from that. Better to just skip the ritual entirely. Just for one night.

"Damn it, Cerys." Winnie laid the candle down on the altar, leaving it on its side, and undressed for bed.

When May was able to stop crying, she went to the bookshelf to retrieve the smudging dish. Her hands shook as she prepared the herbs. She continued to sniffle and occasionally had to wipe the moisture from her eyes with the back of her sleeve. When it was ready, she moved her hands through the smoke and washed it over her head and through her hair. She prayed under her breath as she breathed it in.

Their family wouldn't be in this mess if not for her. Reese often took the brunt of the blame, but the fact was the thread began with May. She fell in love with an older girl, a girl who turned out to be cruel and vicious. Jessica Vaughn. Jessica treated May like a puppy who wouldn't stop following her, and May perfectly played her role of acolyte. She bought small gifts for Jessica, gaudy jewelry and mix tapes, childish tokens of affection.

Eventually Jessica got bored of the little wisp of nothing following her around. But instead of just telling her to scram, Jessica decided to be as brutal as possible.

May picked up the smudging dish and began to move through the room. She spread the smoke slowly along the walls. She stood on chairs to get up into the farthest corners, erasing the harsh language and hurt feelings Winnie and Reese had spilled all over them. She prayed while she did it, her voice trembling with tears she refused to shed.

When Jessica decided she'd had enough of May's affection, she sought out Reese. It was easy to seduce her; Reese was a willing participant since she didn't know how May felt. May was still in the closet at the time so she'd never told Reese or Winnie about her crush. She hadn't been there for the first half of Jessica's endgame, but she knew enough.

Step one: Jessica asks to come over after Reese gets out of school. Winnie will be at work and May will be at their grandmothers' home.

Step two: Ask Reese to kiss her. Turn the kiss into full-blown making out.

Step three: Tell Reese about May's feelings. "I should tell you," Jessica says as Reese is lying under her in a bra and unbuttoned jeans, "that your sister sort of has a crush on me."

"Oh. Is that a problem?" Reese asks, praying it's not.

Jessica drags her fingers down Reese's bare stomach, teasing the fine golden hairs there. "Not for me, if it isn't for you."

Step four: Jessica on her knees, going down on Reese, when May comes home early and walks in on them.

In retrospect, May didn't blame Reese for what happened. No matter how much it hurt, Reese had been temporarily blinded by her lust. She'd been in bed with a beautiful woman who had just half-undressed her, and she was supposed to stop? She was supposed to be thinking clearly when a woman like Jessica Vaughn had one finger on the elastic of her panties? What Reese had done was a betrayal, yes. It stung like hell, but May now believed with all her heart that Reese was as much of a victim as May.

She hoped Winnie would come to the same conclusion about the latest bombshell, but she'd never seen her sister so hurt. She never would have believed Winnie would exile Reese from the family home no matter what her crime. It made her stomach churn and her heart hurt and she realized she was furious with Winnie for what she'd done. In a war between Winnie and Reese, she would always choose Reese. Even if that meant leaving their home and turning her back on Winnie.

And all that combined into the realization that, as frightening as it was to consider, Jessica may have finally succeeded in driving the sisters apart.

CHAPTER ELEVEN

REESE WAS sitting at the foot of the tree in their front yard, the grass soaking the seat of her pants but she was too depressed and angry to care. Depression and anger were odd emotions to feel at the same time. It gelled into some bizarre miasma of sad blankness that made her feel like utter shit. She had nowhere to go. Winnie didn't want her in the house and, after the anger and vitriol dumped on her head, Reese didn't particularly want to spend the night there, either. And she couldn't go to Chloe, because of her damned husband.

The front door to the house opened and May came outside. Reese sat up straighter before she saw the smudging dish in her sister's hand. May crouched and placed the dish on the front step where it would protect their household, then stood and hugged herself. She looked toward the tree knowing she would see Reese sitting there. Her face mirrored Reese's internal conflict.

"I can't let you back in."

"I know," Reese said, just loud enough to be heard across the distance. After storming out, after being banished by Winnie, it would be foolish for May to choose sides. Reese understood that. In her current state of mind, Winnie might not. "Did you smudge?"

May said, "A lot of bad energy in the house. I wouldn't have been able to sleep otherwise."

"Yeah," Reese said. "I'm sorry."

"For what you contributed to the bad energy, or for..."

"For all of it."

May came down off the porch and reached into her pocket. Reese stood and met her halfway, standing on the grass to accept the key. "You can spend the night in Stormy Mouse, if you want. There's that couch in the back. It's not the most comfortable..."

"It's better than any of my other options," Reese said. "Thank you."

May said, "Of course, Rears."

Reese whispered, "Don't call me Rears."

May took her into a hug and kissed her head. Reese burrowed into May's shoulder, her hands gripping the back of May's sweater.

"She really is beautiful," May said. "Do you make each other happy?"

"Yes." Reese was crying now.

May stepped back, cupped Reese's head in her hands, and turned it downward so she could kiss her sister's forehead. Reese put her arms around May's waist. May cradled Reese's head against her shoulder. "I love you, Cerys Aveline. You're my moon and stars."

"I'm in your orbit, Maeve Wren." She wiped her eyes and let May go. "Go. I don't want her to be mad at you, too."

"Well maybe I'm mad at her."

Reese reached up and used her thumb to wipe the moisture from May's cheek. "Go back inside. Take care of her, okay?"

"Okay."

They parted ways. Reese forced herself not to look back when she reached the street. If she looked back and saw Winnie watching from the window, it would be painful to see the anger on her face. But if she looked back and saw the curtain hadn't moved... she wasn't sure she could take that, either. So she kept her eyes forward and held the key so tightly that its teeth dug into the palm of her hand like a blade.

When Winnie was eighteen and her sisters were twelve, they were woken by their mother, Grandy, and Meemaw. The kitchen light had seemed abnormally bright in the pre-dawn darkness as they gathered around the central island. Grandy and Meemaw seemed lit from within, and Ashlyn seemed to be almost as young as her daughters. While they made breakfast - Caprese eggs and marionberry pancakes - the six women danced and sang their favorite songs while Ashlyn made the rounds to spend time with each daughter.

She straightened the wild tangles of Winnie's hair, kissed Reese's freckles, and massaged both of May's hands. At that time, their grandmothers still had an old Labrador named Gavroche, and he lapped the room in a state of ignorant excitement. At one point Ashlyn stooped, grabbed the dog's front paws, and stood him up so she could dance with him around the dining room. Winnie had laughed at the sight but there was concern in her eyes as well. Their mother and grandmothers seemed happy, yes, but there was something manic in their happiness.

Whatever was going to happen, she knew, had equal chance of being terrible and amazing. She wasn't willing to place a bet on which one she thought it would be just yet.

They finished breakfast and the girls were told to put on coats over their pajamas. The elder Cabot women went first, with Winnie following directly behind her mother. Reese and May held hands as the family went out across the lawn. Gavroche came with them, sometimes leading while other times he weaved between them, eager for whatever adventure they might take him on. May looked at the cars they were leaving in the driveway but said nothing. Somehow they all knew they would be walking to wherever they needed to be. It was still dark out. Grandy had a giant old flashlight, a metal cudgel she called a torch, and she led the way down the lane, out of town, and up a hill into the woods.

Ashlyn fell back and put an arm across Winnie's shoulders. Her mania had been left behind in the kitchen and now she seemed focused, serious. She squeezed Winnie against her side.

"Scared?"

"Excited. Nervous." Winnie thought for a moment. "Those are just different words for scared."

Ashlyn nodded. "You can go home if you want. All three of you can go home right now." She looked back at the twins. "Do you want to go back to bed?"

"No ma'am," Reese and May said at the same time Winnie shook her head. They could all feel it now; something important was going to happen. They didn't know what it was, but it felt like they'd been unknowingly waiting for it their entire lives.

Ashlyn rubbed Winnie's arm and faced forward again. "Good girls. That's my girls."

They arrived at a clearing which looked out over the water. A heavy fog bank obscured any hint of the mainland, and the light shining through the veil told them daybreak was only minutes away. The dog, up until then a bundle of energy, walked to a fallen tree at the edge of the clearing and lay down with his head on his paws. Grandy and Meemaw stood with their backs to the cliff. Ashlyn squeezed Winnie's hand once and went to join them. Winnie, Reese, and May faced their elders.

"Listen," Grandy said.

"You can hear it, can't you?" Meemaw asked as seamlessly as if she was the one who had started speaking.

"The island is calling to you," Ashlyn said.

All three spoke together. "When this island rose from the sea, when it was touched by the wind and the air for the first time, a Cabot woman was the first to stand upon its shore. When the first group of townspeople arrived, a Cabot woman helped lay the first foundation. It calls to us, it sings to us, the pulse of the sea against its shore is echoed in our blood."

Ashlyn said, "It is our duty to protect the island."

Grandy said, "It is our privilege to watch over her."

Meemaw said, "It is an honor to speak for her to those who cannot hear."

"The island has a heart," Ashley said, "and we make sure it continues to beat. For twenty years, I've shared that responsibility with my mother and her partner. Today, we pass that honor to you."

Winnie's eyes widened. "Even Cerys and Maeve? They're only little."

Ashlyn smiled. "I was younger than them when my grandmother died. And I know my girls have already felt the powerful energy of this place. I've heard them at night, in their room, practicing spells." The twins looked sheepish, but their mother's smile only widened. "Don't be ashamed. I'm so proud of you both. And I wouldn't be doing this if I thought you were unprepared. You especially, Arwyn. I would say you remind me of myself as a girl, but that would be far too large of a compliment to myself. You are everything I wish I could have been at your age. I'm so proud of you, Winnie."

"Thank you," Winnie said softly. "What do we have to do?"

Meemaw said, "First we have to make sure the little ones are ready as well."

Reese said, "We are."

May reached out and took her sister's hand, implicitly confirming Reese spoke for both of them.

"Okay, then." Meemaw looked at Grandy, the eldest of the gathered women.

"Step into a circle," Grandy said, "Mairwen to my right, then Ashlyn, Arwyn... and I always forget, which twin is the oldest?"

Reese said, "Me... three minutes." She moved to stand next to Winnie, and May closed the circle.

Meemaw smiled at the twins. "Three is a big number in this family. Okay. Join hands. We have to be performing the ritual when the first rays of the sun touch the shore of the island."

They held hands. Grandy began the ritual, speaking just loud enough to be heard, and when the time came for Meemaw and Ashlyn to do their parts, they spoke in the same register. The energy built up around the younger girls who felt it like some unquantifiable joy. It was the feeling of waking up on their birthday mixed with waking up on the first day of school: the glow of importance, happiness, and the weight of responsibility changing the way they experienced the moment.

Winnie gasped. Reese cried. May squeezed Grandy's hand hard enough that, when she eventually let go, she saw a bruise on the back near the pinkie. She apologized profusely and patted the injury as if she could erase it with tenderness. Grandy kissed the top of her granddaughter's head and smoothed her hair before hugging her tight.

"We were all changed tonight, little girl. Sometimes change leaves a mark, that's all."

They walked home as the sun crawled across town. A paperboy spotted them, but even he was old enough to have heard rumors about how the Cabot family was pretty weird. Two fifty-year-olds, their thirty-something daughter, and three of his classmates walking out of the woods in their pajamas mere minutes after dawn wasn't even enough to make him do a double-take. When they got back to the house, Grandy made them pose for a picture on the front porch.

When the flash went off, Grandy patted Winnie on the shoulder. "Everything changes today, girls. Are you sure you're ready?"

May said, "We're ready."

Winnie smiled and nodded. It was a huge responsibility, but she was ready.

Winnie was up before the dawn. On her way down the hall, she noticed May was asleep in Reese's bed. She supposed she shouldn't have been surprised. The house felt hollow without Reese in it. She undressed and took a long shower, head under the cold water in the hopes it would knock out the fever that had built up in the night. She detached the showerhead and aimed it between her legs, using her other hand to find her clit through the spray. She was asexual, and masturbation was just a clinical process for her. Climax felt good, it released endorphins, and eased stress. She liked the way it felt to make herself come but the idea of sharing this ritual with another person disgusted her. She would just as soon let someone watch her go to the bathroom.

Afterward, she was relaxed but the turmoil in her head hadn't lessened. She put on a sleeveless silk top and baggy slacks and went to sit on the back steps. She couldn't see the water from there but she could smell it. She could see the dew glistening on the grass. People at the nearby houses loudly prepared for school and work, passing down the alley in pajama pants as a leashed dog tugged them along.

Winnie brought her hand to her lips and blew air between two fingers. It was cold enough for her exhalation to become a small wisp of smoke. It hardened at her touch, and she began to bend and twist it into spirals. When it became tangled she pinched and let it dissolve. She blew again to make another spear and began to manipulate it as well. It was a poor use of energy, but it kept her mind and hands occupied without resorting to cigarettes or electronics.

May came outside fully dressed, in black slacks and a periwinkle blouse, no tie. She sat down next to Winnie and watched as she played with the piece of fog. She reached out and plucked it away from her, then brought it to her lips and swallowed it with a single sharp inhale. She kept her lips shut tight and pulled her knees in close so she could wrap her arms around them.

"Do you hate me?" Winnie asked.

"I'm angry at you," May said, then immediately revised it with, "I'm furious with you. And disappointed. I don't hate you, Arwyn."

Winnie wiped away a tear and nodded, still not looking at her sister. "I don't even know where she spent the night."

"I do," May said.

She didn't elaborate, and Winnie knew that was part of her

punishment. She accepted that.

"I have to go somewhere before I go to work. So I'm not going to have breakfast with you. I'll probably see you for dinner, though."

Winnie nodded. She didn't trust herself to speak.

"We're going to be okay," May said. "We're the Cabot girls. If we don't have each other, what do we have?" She blew out a ribbon of air, hardened it, and cupped it in her hands to mold it into a heart. She handed it to Winnie, who carefully held it between two fingers. "I'm mad at you and I spent last night crying because of you, and I hurt in a way I never thought you could make me hurt. But I can feel all of that and still love you. You're my Winnie."

"I love you, too," Winnie said.

May stood up and walked away across the yard. When she was gone, Winnie closed her eyes and pressed the stolen breath against her cheek until it melted.

It wasn't quite the same as the goodbye kiss her sister had neglected to give her, but given the circumstances, it was more than enough.

CHAPTER TWELVE

MAY LEFT her bicycle next to the porch and walked across town, taking the time to organize her thoughts. She'd lain awake most of the night going over the explosion from the night before. She only got to sleep after going through the curtain and sleeping in Reese's bed. When she woke up, the jumbled memories of the fight had settled into an orderly arrangement and she saw something that shook her more than Winnie and Reese's feud. It was a theory which, if true, could further destroy their family.

But she had to know for certain. So her feet continued to carry her up the hill to her grandmothers' house where she could ask a question while dreading she already knew the answer.

May let herself in through the front door; the island was small enough that few people bothered to lock up. Every room but the kitchen was dark and the furniture looked like set pieces waiting for a play to begin. The radio was playing static with a weak signal of music valiantly trying to make it through. May maneuvered through the quiet rooms like a ghost and stopped when she reached the threshold of light.

Grandy was at the cutting board with her back to the room but she spoke as if she not only knew who her guest was, but had been expecting her.

"We can still cut up our own bananas and pour our own coffee, you know. We don't need you for every meal."

May said, "I know."

Grandy turned around, concerned by the tone of May's voice. "What's wrong, dear?"

"I..." She closed her mouth tightly around whatever words might follow. She fussed with the hem of her shirt and, for want of something to do, began tucking it in.

"You're dressed like a boy again." Grandy turned back to finish preparing her food.

"I dress like this all the time, Grandy. Either get used to it or stop saying anything."

Grandy turned slowly this time. "What's gotten into you?"

May took a deep, slow breath. "Last night, we found out Reese is sleeping with a married woman. Someone gave Winnie pictures that proved it. I was so shocked by the pictures that I didn't think about them too hard, but something about them st-stuck out to me. They were sepia. Orange-brown. Old." She swallowed the lump in her throat. "I've only seen pictures like that here. In your home. So either someone was using your camera... or..."

"There are plenty of old cameras in the world, Maeve. Before you were born, they were the only kind that existed."

"Don't lie to me."

"I'm not lying, I'm just saying~"

"It's the *same fucking thing*," May snapped.

Grandy betrayed no shock from May's outburst. She put her banana peel in the bag for composting and wiped her hands together. "No one told your sister to sleep with a married woman, Maeve. Secrets hide in the dark and gather dust, and the dust grows into mountains. All I did was turn on the light to clean things up a little."

"And what about when we were teenagers?" May said.

Grandy's hand stalled on the way to the cupboard. "What about what?"

May was crying silently now. "I never thought about it because that day was always about what I saw when I got home. What I walked in on. But last night, I was thinking. Jessica Vaughn gave Winnie the pictures. And Jessica Vaughn also tried to get between us when we were teenagers, for no real reason. Just to be cruel, I thought. But her plan doesn't make sense, Grandy. Her plan doesn't make sense because she was having sex with Reese when I was supposed to be here. Making you and Meemaw dinner. That's why Reese thought it was safe. I went straight home from school that day because you called. You said you and Meemaw were going out to dinner that night and I didn't need to come by."

Grandy put her hand down. She still wasn't looking at May.

"It never occurred to me that you were part of her plan, because I couldn't believe you would hurt me like that on purpose. But now I know that it couldn't have worked without your help. Why?"

"I've always been practical," Grandy said slowly. "I've always looked at the whole board before making my move."

May whispered, "Always take the money on game shows. Never the prizes."

"The prizes, you have to pay taxes on them and then you have to worry about transporting them, and if it's a dadgum game room or something, well, hell, where are you supposed to put it?" She sighed and finally faced her granddaughter. "You and your sisters are supposed to watch over this island. Protect it. Be the custodians of its energy. You've been doing a good job for the most part. But one responsibility has fallen by the wayside."

"We've done everything asked of us. The rituals, the spells..."

"Yes, yes, that's fine. That's fine. But my darling girl, you're a gay virgin. Winnie is an asexual, whatever that means. It's a whole thing these days, I guess, everyone wants their own special category."

May said, "What does my virginity have to do with..." Her eyes widened. "Oh."

"There have always been Cabot girls on Coventry Island," Grandy said calmly. "Ideally, there are three, but that's not a requirement. And if one of you had been born male, we would have done our best. But my love, Arwyn is almost in her forties, at which point having a child will start to be very uncertain. Cerys claims to be bisexual but keeps throwing herself crotch-first at women. At the wrong women, most times. And then there's you."

"You broke my heart, you might have destroyed Winnie and Reese's relationship forever, just because I won't get laid? Just because I haven't had a baby?"

"You're running out of time, Maeve. We're running out of time. You run your little shop and Winnie sells her cookies, but what happens when you're gone? What happens when you want to pass the torch? Mairwen and I won't be around much longer, I'm sorry to say, and it wouldn't be fair to ask your mother to take up the responsibility again."

May wiped away her tears with her sleeve. "We weren't too old when we were teenagers. We still had lots of time to have babies or start a family. Why did you stand in the way then?"

Grandy looked at the floor and ran her tongue over her teeth, making a lump in her upper lip. "Because I looked ahead. I saw what might have been if you didn't get over your crush on Jessica Vaughn. She would have seen you as you are. Sincere. Pure. She would have been changed by your love of her. She was going to return your love. But she was always destined to leave the island and, when she did, she would have taken you with her."

May gasped, a sharp and broken sound. "No..."

"What we did..."

"Shut up!" May shrieked. "You told us this was a responsibility, but that's not what you meant. You meant it was a prison."

Grandy stepped forward, angry now. "No! This is an honor. To build your life around something greater than yourself~"

May swiped her hand through the air and Grandy's mouth snapped shut. "I told you to stop talking, you *witch*."

Grandy's eyes flashed with anger at the word being slung at her like a slur.

"Horrible hag," May sobbed. "Cursing your own flesh and blood. My life. My whole life. I've been waiting to find love. *You stole it from me?*" She spread her fingers. "You will not speak again until I allow it. Your voice is mine, you wretched thing, and I will bury it deep in the darkest cave where you can never find it."

A light came on elsewhere in the house. "Maeve? Eliza, what's~"

May reached out her other hand in the direction of Meemaw's voice and curled her fingers, then pulled. A door upstairs slammed shut hard enough to shake the walls. She never took her eyes off Grandy.

"I will restore your voice only for you to mend the relationship between Arwyn Mavis and Cerys Aveline Cabot. But even on that day, you are never to speak to me again. Never. The damage you've done to me cannot be undone, and for that your punishment will be unending. I hate you, Eliza May Cabot. I hate you as I've never hated any person and hope to never hate another. These will be the last words I ever direct at you. You are not forgiven, witch, and I hate you. Goodbye."

She turned and moved through the house. The furniture she passed trembled and scooted away from her, unmoored by the force of the energy coursing through her. She held out her hand, punched the front door open without touching it, and left the house without breaking stride. Meemaw came around the corner of the house as May crossed the lawn. The hem of her nightgown was wet where it was being dragged through the grass.

"Maeve! Maeve, please!"

May pretended she couldn't hear her and continued walking, eyes on the trees at the end of the property. She knew Meemaw wouldn't follow her that far so she just had to get there first.

Beyond that, she had no plan whatsoever.

Ashlyn Cabot slept through her alarm for the first time in over a decade. The amount of light in her bedroom confused her when she finally opened her eyes and it took her a moment to realize what had happened. The store had already missed the first group of tourists and was close to missing the second as well. When she got out of bed she stepped on her belt buckle, cutting her foot. The hot water cut out in the middle of her shower. She ripped her blouse when she put it on. By the time she got out the door, she half expected a plane to fall out of the sky and crush her.

On the drive through town, she noticed that Stormy Mouse and Will & Winn were both closed. A cluster of customers were standing outside the door of Winnie's bakery, milling about anxiously as they waited for the doors to open. Ashlyn pressed her lips together in a tight line and continued to her shop. She opened up and went to the phone in her office to dial her mothers. Mairwen picked up on the first ring and began speaking even before Ashlyn could ask.

"Your daughter has gone insane."

"What? Mom, what's happening?"

Mairwen said, "I woke up this morning because I heard shouting. I tried to go downstairs but the door slammed in my face. I had to go out the window and jump down to the lawn." Ashlyn was momentarily distracted by the image of her mother performing these acrobatics, which sounded impressive even with the assistance of magic. "I could hear Maeve shouting at Eliza even from outside. She called her a witch, Ash."

"Maeve did? What on earth would make her do that?" She could see Reese getting that angry, and in extreme circumstances, even Winnie. But May was such a sweetheart that she would apologize to people who bumped into her.

"I don't know, because Eliza can't speak. May cursed her. Took away her voice?"

Ashlyn's mouth hung open. "My Maeve would never do that."

"She did. You can come over here and see it for yourself. The girl was out of control."

After a moment's consideration, Ashlyn went back to the front door and locked it again. The closed storefronts were now alarming clues that something was very, very wrong with her daughters. She could miss a day of sales if the girls needed her.

"Where is May now?"

"I don't know. She went off into the woods and I couldn't follow her. My knees... and I was worried about Eliza."

"I understand. Take care of her. I'll go find the girls. I'll fix this."

She hung up and went back out to her car. The entire drive to her daughters' home, she tried and failed to envision May doing what Mairwen accused her of. She couldn't even imagine May raising her voice let alone using a slur or wielding magic as a weapon. A curse... from Maeve? It was more plausible to imagine possession or a shapeshifter on the island.

Winnie was sitting on the back steps when Ashlyn pulled up. Her eldest daughter didn't move, didn't look away from the distant point she'd locked her focus on, and for a moment Ashlyn feared she was also under some spell.

"Arwyn?" she said quietly.

"Hi, mommy." Her voice was small, diminished, and she kept her eyes focused on distant nothing.

She hid her relief and crouched so their faces were lined up. "Arwyn... your grandmother just told me something very troubling. Do you know anything about it?"

Winnie's eyes were wet with tears. She nodded slowly. Ashlyn reached out and took her hand.

"Honey, what... what on earth would make her do that?"

"She said she fell in love."

Ashlyn narrowed her eyes. "May fell in love with someone...?"

Winnie finally looked at her mother. "What? No. Reese. What did May do?"

"She attacked your grandmother."

Winnie's eyes flashed like fire. "What?" She stood up and Ashlyn rose with her. "Is she okay? Meemaw or Grandy? What the hell happ-- May? May attacked her?"

"She attacked Grandy," Ashlyn said. "Meemaw said she was

fine, she's just... she... she was cursed. She can't speak."

"Maeve cursed Grandy?" Winnie's voice was small. The tears finally fell free. "Everything's broken. We're broken. Where is May now?"

"We don't know. I was hoping you and Cerys could help find her."

Winnie laughed bitterly. "We... we don't know where Reese is. May knew. But she wouldn't tell me. She's mad at me because I exiled Reese last night."

Ashlyn thought perhaps she was the one who had been cursed, that she'd woken up in some hollow and false world that looked like her home but operated under different rules.

"You exiled Reese? What... wh-what do you mean, darling?"

"I kicked her out of the house. She had an affair with a married woman. Just like daddy."

Ashlyn closed her eyes. "Oh, goddess." She put her fingers over her mouth and turned to look down the street. Her foot throbbed where she'd cut it, and she remembered all the mishaps that morning. No wonder everything felt off-kilter. No wonder the ground felt uneven beneath her. Winnie, Reese, and May were fractured, May and Winnie had both lashed out at their own flesh and blood, and now half the Cabot family was missing or cut off from the others.

For the first time in recorded history, the protection offered by the Cabot bloodline was fractured, and the island was more vulnerable than it had ever been before.

She prayed it could survive until things were put right.

CHAPTER THIRTEEN

MAY REACHED the shore. She stood with her feet in the water, looked to her right, and saw the docks. She saw the trappings of town, the only civilization on the island. She let the waves lap over her ankles once - a single beat of the island's pulse - and turned to her left.

She began to walk.

CHAPTER FOURTEEN

REESE DIDN'T sleep enough to be confused by her surroundings when she woke up. She planned to lie down on the couch in their back room so she could at least try to sleep, but instead she wandered the dark store for most of the night. She sat in the front window and stared out at the empty streets. Streetlights on either end of the block shone bright blue-white, the one to the south flickering slightly. Reese let it hypnotize her as her mind wandered.

She thought of Chloe at home with Lucas. Comfortable and warm in her house, tucked into her own bed. It was unfair. It was almost cruel for Reese to be suffering the consequences when Chloe was the adulterer. A dark part of her brain wanted to even the score by heading over and spilling the beans. It would make them miserable but at least they could keep each other warm.

In the morning light, she knew she would never have gone through with something so cruel. Especially not to someone she loved as much as Chloe. But it was most likely only a matter of time before the truth came out. Either Jessica would whisper in the wrong ear or Winnie would somehow let it slip just to "balance the energies" of the universe.

Winnie. Stupid, moral, black-and-white Winnie. Just because their father had broken the family and their mother's heart, adultery was inexcusable in Winnie's eyes. But Chloe was miserable in her marriage. If Winnie could have seen how lost Chloe was that first day... or how she'd changed in the time they'd been sleeping together...

She held her left hand out and moved the fingers of her right hand over the palm. Energy sparked and danced as if she was holding a raincloud.

"Look through my eyes and see what I've seen. You know my heart now see my soul. Understand where I've been."

Reese moved her hands apart and the energy scattered unfocused. She wanted Winnie to truly see and understand her. Why was that so unreasonable?

"Your sister is happy." She cupped her hand over her eyes. "Why does it matter who it's with?"

Winnie accepted her as bisexual, and she had no problem with May being a lesbian. But because Chloe happened to have made a mistake in the past and married the wrong man, they had to be punished. They had to be shunned and forced apart.

Reese pushed herself up and went to the racks. She refused. She wouldn't let the best woman she'd ever known slip through her fingers. If it meant she had to break ties with Winnie, then... then maybe it was time to leave the nest. She was in her thirties, she was an adult, and maybe the days of sharing a bedroom with her twin sister were behind her.

She took a clean blouse and slacks off the rack and went into the small bathroom next to the office. She washed up as best she could, put on the new clothes, and locked the back door when she left the shop. May would probably be in soon and wonder where she was, but she didn't want to put off her mission. She needed to see Chloe again, kiss her, hold her, remind herself of what she was suffering for. Once she'd done that she would be ready for round two of her confrontation with Winnie.

Chloe and her husband lived one block removed from the edge of town. From their backyard, they could see the docks and hear the rumble of engines when people were waiting to be taken back to the mainland. Reese had never spent the night there, but she'd visited often enough that she didn't have to doublecheck the address. She loitered on the corner to make sure Chloe's car was the only one in the driveway before she risked approaching.

She went around to the side door and knocked, staying close to the wall in case any nosy neighbors happened to look out.

Chloe answered the door still in plaid pajama bottoms and a

white T-shirt. Her hair was still wet from the shower. Reese was caught momentarily speechless; all the time they'd been together and she'd never seen the woman she loved on a normal, domestic morning. The realization hurt, but it also helped convince her she'd done the right thing. This was the woman she loved. She'd slept around, she'd had girlfriends, but in the end, even if she lost everything else, she would always have—

"You cannot be here," Chloe snapped, countering her words by pulling Reese into the house. They were in a small laundry room off the kitchen. The dryer rumbled and rattled behind them. "We talked about this, Reese. Lucas might have been home."

"I looked for his car before I even came down the street."

"That doesn't make this okay." She took a breath and noted the unwashed hair and redness in her eyes. Her anger faded and she put her hands on Reese's shoulders. "Baby, what happened?"

Reese just barely stopped herself from crying. "Winnie and May know. They found out. Someone gave Winnie some pictures."

Chloe bit down on a gasp, eyes widening with fear. "Are they going to show Lucas?"

"No," Reese said, "and I'm fine, by the way."

"Of course I'm worried about you, too," Chloe said, "but you don't—"

Reese waved her off. "Forget it. Winnie has as much to lose as you do. Your husband could shut down her bakery just to get back at my family."

"Come in here."

Chloe guided Reese through the kitchen into the main house. The living room always felt cramped, small and overstuffed with furniture and bookshelves. There was no television but a telescope stood next to the window. On the far wall, above the divan where Reese spent an afternoon pushing Chloe to the edge and then pulling her back, a Vanessa Kavik landscape provided the sole splash of color under a trio of bullet-shaped picture lights. Reese took a seat under the painting and Chloe perched on the edge of the couch beside her.

"Tell me what happened."

"Winnie kicked me out. I told you how she feels about adultery. I thought maybe she would feel differently because it was me, but I guess..." She looked down at her hands. "May couldn't take my side or she probably would have gotten kicked out, too. I slept at the store last night. I mean, I spent the night there. I didn't really sleep."

Chloe reached up and touched Reese's hair. "I'm so sorry."

"I know you have to get to work, but I kind of hoped I could just use your shower. I'll lock up when I leave."

"Oh. I... I would say yes, Reese, but Lucas sometimes comes home during the day. He has a strange schedule."

Reese said, "Forget it."

Chloe said, "I just don't know how I would explain it if he found you in the shower."

"Why not the truth? Winnie and May know. Jessica Vaughn knows."

"Who is Jessica Vaughn?"

Reese shook her head. "It's not important. People know now. I'm willing to bet Winnie is going to tell Mom and my grandmothers."

Chloe said, "A family secret isn't the same as Lucas finding out. It's more complicated than that." She slipped her hand away from Reese's shoulder. "Winnie has incentive to keep Lucas from finding out. He would ruin her business, same as he would ruin mine. What you're suggesting is just... it's... bringing the worst case scenario to life."

Reese stared at her. "So what are you saying?"

"I'm saying this doesn't have to be the worst possible outcome."

"You mean I don't have to take you down with me."

Chloe squeezed her eyes shut. "No. No, that is not what I'm saying, Cerys."

"You want to stay married to him. You want this all to just go away." She stood up and held out her hands to indicate herself. "Look at me, Chloe. This is already the worst possible outcome for me. I have nowhere to go. I thought you were the one place on the island I could go for comfort and understanding, but if keeping your sham marriage~"

"Hey."

"What? You're offended? He's sleeping with someone else, and you claim to be in love with me. Sorry for insulting your vows."

Chloe stood up as well. "Reese, if this was simple~"

"Seems pretty simple to me. You have an affair and somehow I lose everything. Seems pretty cut and dry from where I'm sitting."

"You haven't lost everything. You still have me."

"You *literally* just told me I couldn't even use your shower,

Chloe. I come to you for comfort and solace and you give me a pat on the shoulder before sending me on my way. Not only have I lost you, I don't think I ever really had you in the first place."

Chloe said, "Reese, I love you."

"No, you don't." She turned and walked back to the laundry room. "You love convenience. You love your garage. You love the life you had, and you're not willing to risk any of that to help me."

Chloe caught up with Reese and wrapped both arms around her waist. She dropped to her knees, put her head against the curve of Reese's lower back, and squeezed.

"Don't leave me. I'm scared, Cerys, I'm so scared. My job and my marriage and this house are things I need to feel safe and secure. You're the only thing I want. The only part of my whole life that I chose for myself. You're the most precious thing in my life. But I'm so scared to be broke and adrift. I'm so terrified of that, Reese. Just because I'm weak doesn't mean you're unimportant. You kept me alive for so long. You are the only reason I wake up some mornings. Please, Cerys, don't. Don't go."

Reese pulled Chloe's hands loose. "You say I'm you're everything, but you're only offering me a fraction of you. One tiny little piece. It's not enough anymore, Chloe. Maybe it never was." She put her hand on the doorknob and hesitated. "Tell me to stay. Right now, tell me I can take a shower and nap on your couch. That would honestly be enough."

Chloe took a long time to respond. "I can't."

"Goodbye, Chloe. Thanks for ruining my life for no goddamn reason."

"Reese!"

She went outside and slammed the door behind her. She was vaguely aware of small animals - cats and squirrels and birds - fleeing from her path as she walked, but none of them registered. They could feel the rage, hurt, and heartbreak brewing inside her and moved as quickly as they could to get out of its way. She didn't know where she was going. There was literally nowhere on the island where she felt she would be welcomed.

Nowhere on the island. That settled it.

She went to the docks and was relieved to see Barty was already there. Cars were being loaded onto his lower deck, but she walked up the ramp that took her past the bridge. He saw her coming and stepped out.

"Cerys Cabot. Don't hardly see you taking to the mainland..."

He pushed the brim of his cap up and stared harder at her. "Miss Cabot, you okay? You look a little peaky."

"I need to go," Reese said. "I don't have money for a ticket."

"That's fine," Barty said, now sounding truly concerned. "Hon, I think you might want to stay home today. I can call Arwyn~"

Reese said, "I'm leaving."

"Okay. Okay." He backed away from her and looked at the sky. "Don't know where this storm came from all'a sudden, though..."

Reese looked up and saw thick, dark clouds clustering overhead. The waves were choppy as well, and she knew her foul mood was seeping out into the world. She walked to the edge of the deck and placed her hands on the railing. Her fingers were trembling and pale. She closed her eyes and took a series of long, deep breaths which she let out through her nose. She focused her swirling emotions just enough to ensure they would have safe passage to the mainland.

The horn blew and the boat pulled away from the dock just as the first fat droplets of icy rain splattered against Reese's cheeks, indiscernible from the tear tracks already there.

CHAPTER FIFTEEN

THE HOUSE felt dead, cold, and empty when Winnie woke up. She was almost used to it by now. It was the second morning she'd woken up without the sound of May's shower or Reese calling up to ask what they wanted for breakfast. Her altar stood untouched in the corner. She sat on the edge of her bed and stared accusingly at the abandoned cloth and unburnt candles. No word from either of her sisters, no sign of them anywhere on the island. Grandy was still mute from May's spell, and every time Winnie tried to make sense of that, her mind rebelled. May, striking out in anger, doing the kind of witchcraft they'd always sworn was off-limits. What could have prompted her to take that step?

Fortunately the karmic balance had restored itself enough that she didn't have to worry about harming herself during her morning routine. No electric shocks from the coffee maker and no busted pipe soaking her when she started the laundry. She had washed everything in May and Reese's hampers. The clothes stood folded and stacked neatly on the dryer, waiting for their owners to put it all away. Ashlyn had floated the idea that they might not be coming back, but Winnie couldn't think like that. Not yet.

She walked to the Passoth's garage and let herself into the office. She didn't have to wait long before someone saw her and passed along word to Chloe she had a guest. The mechanic arrived a few minutes later. She looked haggard and distraught as she took a seat behind her desk. She avoided Winnie's eyes and focused on the desktop.

"Do you know where she--"

"Is my truck ready?" Winnie asked.

Chloe said, "Yeah. It needed--"

"I don't care. How much do I owe you?"

"I had the parts already." Her voice was small, her head moving slowly from side to side. "There's no charge."

Winnie took out her wallet. "I don't want to owe you anything, and I don't want you thinking this covers any kind of debt. How much?"

Chloe said, "Fine. A dollar."

Winnie tossed a twenty on the desk. "Keep the change."

"Arwyn..."

She was out the door before Chloe could say anything else. She went to her truck, climbed behind the wheel, and realized she didn't have the keys just as Chloe caught up with her.

"Your fucking keys," Chloe said, throwing them into the truck past Winnie. "I made a mistake. But that mistake wasn't falling in love with your sister, it was falling in love with her too late. I was lazy when I was younger. I wanted everything handed to me, and Lucas offered me whatever I wanted in return for a wedding ring. Seemed like a pretty sweet deal. He didn't set off fireworks for me, but none of the men on the island really did. Why not him? Then I met Reese and found out why I never felt fireworks before. I didn't know how to just torpedo the rest of my life for her even when I admitted I wanted to. I couldn't divorce Lucas for the same reason you haven't told him about the affair. He gives us everything we want but with the threat it could be taken away if we make him angry."

Winnie retrieved her keys and jabbed them into the ignition. "I don't care about your justifications."

"I wanted to end the marriage before Reese and I became friends. I was trapped even before I knew there was something to run to. She gave me a reason to wake up in the morning. To keep going."

"Step back or I'm going to run over your foot."

Chloe stayed where she was for a moment but then moved away from the truck. Winnie checked behind her and reversed out of the garage.

At Will & Winn, she parked in her usual spot and went in

through the kitchen so she wouldn't have to see any customers. She couldn't deal with their smiling faces or attempts at conversation. She needed to be in her private space. Clark the baker saw her first, in the cramped area between her office and the employee lockers. He gave a look of such fear and surprise that she initially thought she'd caught him doing something illegal. But he glanced over his shoulder and moved out of her way as she barreled through. Apparently her behavior the past two days had taught her employees not to cross her.

Or at least that was what she thought. When she entered the kitchen, she stopped at the edge of the non-slip rubber mats and stared at what was happening.

Florence, the lanky high school girl who usually worked out front, was standing over several rows of finished baked goods. Her hands were out, her head bowed, her black curls bundled into a ball at the base of her skull. Winnie could feel scraps of energy around the girl but it was a pathetic breeze compared to how true power would have felt.

"What the hell do you think you're doing?"

Florence jumped and spun around. She grabbed at the table to keep from falling over and knocked one tray of cookies onto the floor. The magic in the air fizzled to nothing as the tray rattled and clattered until it finally came to rest. Clark had come back but was lingering by the door so as not to get between the two women. Florence glanced toward the kitchen door and Winnie understood someone at the counter was supposed to have warned her when she arrived.

"Answer me," Winnie said.

"I just... thought... I was just trying something different."

Winnie said, "What the hell gave you the right?"

"I was wrong," Florence said. "I know that. I admit it. But I... I know you've been going through some stuff with your sisters. The whole island probably knows it by now. I was just trying to take some of the burden off of you."

"What I'm going through with my sisters has nothing to do with my ability to work."

Florence glanced at Clark for help. He didn't offer it. "Winnie... Miss Cabot... with all due respect, there ha-have been some complaints."

Winnie furrowed her brow. "Complaints about what?"

"The cookies. The bread, the coffee, the cupcakes. Everything, really."

Clark said, "People have said they taste like shit the past couple of days."

Winnie spun toward him. He cringed.

Florence said, "I have some power. It's nothing like you or your family. But some. Enough, maybe, that I could've covered for you until this whole... th-this whatever is happening... until it passed and you were yourself again."

Winnie looked at the spilled tray of cookies, her eyes skimming back to Florence. "Get out."

"Right. I'll just go back out–"

"I'll mail your last paycheck."

Florence stopped at the door. "Wait. What? You're firing me?"

"You overstepped your responsibilities, you insulted the quality of our product, and destroyed a whole batch of cookies. That's unacceptable. Three strikes in the space of five minutes. I want you gone."

Florence's eyes flooded. "But... I... I thought..."

"Miss Cabot, she was only trying to help. Besides, I was the one who insulted the quality. You want to fire me, too?"

"Don't tempt me."

Clark reached behind his back to untie his apron. "You know what, if this is the way things are going to be around here, I can find work somewhere else."

Florence said, "Clark, don't quit for me..."

"I'm not. I'm quitting because I don't want to hang out on a sinking ship." He looked at Winnie. "You're a good lady. A great boss. If you get past whatever this is, I hope you'll come to your senses about what happened this morning. I hope you realize we were just trying to help you. If not, then it was nice knowing you, Miss Cabot."

She watched them leave, fuming, and then went back out into the main room. There were only a handful of customers sitting in the booths, but a long line of tourists were waiting at the counter. Two clerks were at the counter trying to choose between staring at her and watching as Clark and Florence made their way to the door.

"Which one of you were supposed to warn her I was coming?" Winnie asked.

One of them, Meg, said, "Miss Cabot, what's–"

"Fine. You're both fired, too. Get the hell out of my store." She looked at the waiting customers and raised her voice. "We're closed. Everyone get out."

There was a brief murmur of confusion, but the customers began milling toward the exit. Meg was still behind the counter as the last people left. Winnie glared at her, but the other woman stood her ground.

"Arwyn? What's going on? You look ill."

"I'm going to be fine," Winnie said. "I told you to get out of my store."

She didn't wait to see if Meg complied. She turned and went into the kitchen, letting the door swing shut behind her.

Winnie stood in the silent kitchen and focused on the movement of her shoulders with each sharp inhale, every ragged exhale. Her face was hot, both hands fisted in rage, and she realized she didn't recognize herself. The sounds of her own body were wrong. Her breath didn't sound like that. Her face was never this tight. Her hands never hurt from the act of clenching them into fists. She let out a noise like a wounded animal and backed up as if she could retreat from the thing she'd become. Her back hit the fridge and she sank to the floor.

"Cerys," she whispered, covering her face with both hands. "Oh, goddess, Cerys."

Outside she could hear her staff - probably former staff, as they would be completely in their rights to never come back after what she'd done - talking to the customers. Telling them the store has to close for the day. Apologizing. She hears the words "family emergency" unaware that it's closer to the truth than they know.

When her father cheated, she was just old enough to understand the implications of what she was overhearing. She knew what sex was even if the topic didn't interest her. The pain in her mother's voice was still clear even from the top of the stairs. She had her knees up and her arms wrapped around them, staring at the wallpaper as the unthinkable happened downstairs. Her parents were happy. Her parents were unbreakable and forever.

"And what about the girls?" her mother asked.

"This has nothing to do with them."

"You're their *father*, it certainly does have something to do with them. How do you think they'll feel when you're suddenly gone?"

Her father said, "I'm not going anywhere."

"Oh, you certainly are. You're not staying in this house. I won't share a bed with someone who would treat me with such disregard. If you were bored, you should have asked."

He laughed. "Oh, and you would have granted permission to let me sleep around?"

"I'd rather live with a happy, satisfied husband than someone who would deceive me, who would lie to my face while he acted selfishly. You treated me like a fool but worse, you treated me like the enemy. Any partnership we may have had ended when you cut me out. I didn't decide we were over. You decided it. I want you out of this house tonight."

Silence fell. Winnie was crying silently so she wouldn't be heard and sent to bed, but she could almost picture her parents standing on opposite ends of the living room.

"My things?"

"I'll have the girls spend the night with their grandmothers. You can come then. Whatever you can take in one night is yours. Everything else... you can do without."

He sighed heavily. "We could get through this, Ash. You know that."

"Leave."

The door opened and closed. Winnie went to bed and, later on, she heard her mother smudging the house.

That was the day Winnie learned cheating was unforgiveable. It was also the last day she'd seen her father. He'd committed the ultimate sin and his punishment was exile. And now she'd lain down the same sentence on Reese. Had she really seen her sister for the final time? That thought made her shiver and she put her hands on the sides of her head, fingers linked at the back of her skull.

The kitchen door opened and Florence came back inside. She stood for a long moment just inside the threshold of the kitchen.

"I'm not taking anything you say right now as a final decision," Florence finally said, her voice firm but wavering. "I know I messed up, Winnie. I do. This is your area and I should never have taken your job without talking to you first. But we've been through too much together for me to just walk away. So I'm going to take a few days. Then I'll come back. And if you still want me gone, I'll hand in my apron and my company shirts–" Her voice broke then. "I'll quit so you don't have to pay me severance. I hope it won't come to that, though."

Winnie looked up at her. "I'm sorry, Florence."

"I know."

Florence left and Winnie drew her knees up to her chest, just as she had all those years ago. Her mother had drawn a line in the sand all those years ago, and their family had never been the same. But in the end, they had not only survived but grown stronger in his absence.

Winnie could only hope what happened next was for the best as well.

CHAPTER SIXTEEN

Three Days Later

REESE WAS starting to get used to the women's shelter. When she got to Shield, she got in the first bus heading west and rode until she found a town of reasonable size. Owl Lake looked like an insignificant cluster of buildings from the road, but she'd known well enough to look past the façade. Streets meandered and fractured out from each other. Houses sat on sprawling lots that were mostly hidden by trees. There was a school, a post office, at least three churches of various faiths. Reese wandered until she found the place she believed had been calling to her: the women's shelter.

It was a former church, a concrete block with crosses carved on the doors and bunks set up in the former Sunday school classrooms. The lawn was overgrown but otherwise seemed cared-for, and efforts had been taken to make the white fence around the back lawn look presentable.

The shelter's director, Sarah Kirkland, happened to be outside working on a car when Reese came across the parking lot. It was hard to tell how tall she was while under the hood, but the angle of her back and the set of her hips implied she was at least Reese's height if not taller. She paused her work but didn't rise from the engine when Reese approached to ask if they had any available space. She wasn't hopeful; she may have had nothing and nowhere to go, but she still didn't think it was right to take up room at the shelter. She wasn't fleeing an abusive husband and she wasn't technically homeless, but she had nowhere else to go. She had to explore the option even if it meant being turned away.

Sarah listened to Reese's story and, when it was finished, said, "We don't cater exclusively to abused women. Do you think you're above needing our help?"

"No. Goddess, no, not at all. I just worry there are too many women in worse situations and not enough room."

"There are a lot of women who need us," Sarah acknowledged. She straightened and wiped her hands on a rag. "What we don't have is hands to go around. If you want to feel like you're doing more than just taking up space, we can use the help."

Reese agreed. Sarah took her inside to show her around.

"Are you having car trouble?"

Sarah looked back at the car. "No. Jack Sommers was. He donated the car to us, and I'm seeing if I can get it running again. Do you know anything about cars?"

"Sorry, no."

"That's okay. We have plenty of other work for you."

Sarah put Reese to work in a small bedroom where donated clothes, shoes, makeup, and toiletries needed to be sorted. Reese told her that she worked at a thrift shop and she would feel right at home with the task. So far she had spent both days of her residency folding and hanging clothes according to size. She blessed each item with serenity and a sense of protection in the hopes it would do more than clothe those in need.

There were four beds to every room, and one had been empty every night she'd been there. If there came a time when they were full to capacity, she would sleep on the floor of Sarah's office. She woke on the third morning and looked around the room, still expecting to see May. Her current "roommates" had already woken up and left for the day. She was sharing space with a woman in her twenties with tattoos across her shoulders and a woman in her late thirties who arrived with her seven-year-old son. They were in the sanctuary where a small computer bank gave them a place to check their email, look for work, or get in touch with people who could help them make a permanent escape.

Reese went into the kitchen to make two plates of eggs, bacon, sausage, and hash browns. She took the plates to director's office, where she found Sarah nursing a tepid cup of coffee.

"That's not technically a breakfast."

"It's close enough for me." She perked up when she saw what Reese was carrying. "I can be persuaded to change my mind, though."

Reese said, "Don't make assumptions. Both of these are for me. I'm ravenous."

Sarah grinned and took one of the plates. She pushed her laptop aside with one hand to put it down in front of her. Reese sat across from her.

"How are you adjusting to the shelter?"

"What adjust?" Reese asked. "I live with my two sisters with one and a half bathroom, so I'm no stranger to a crowd at all hours."

Sarah said, "You're using the present tense, you know. You *live* with your sisters, not used to live. Does that mean you feel there's an opening to go back?"

Reese considered the question as she poked her eggs. "I don't know. They're my family. I've literally known them my whole life, and I can't imagine a life without them in it. But Winnie... and then May. I understand why May didn't stand up for me. If she had, she'd probably be right here with me. I wanted her to stay. She can be at home with our grandparents and the store. But that doesn't make it hurt any less. If we do settle this and I get to go home, will I think about this every time I look at her? Will I ever not remember her shutting the door on me?"

"I don't know," Sarah said. "You'll have to decide for yourself how much forgiveness you can give her."

"I'm not sure she needs any. I was in the wrong. I've always thought cheaters had a whole level of Hell to themselves. I saw what cheating did to my parents. And I swore I'd never let anyone get away with cheating on me." She chuckled softly and shook her head. "We never imagine ourselves as the cheaters, do we?"

"Mm," Sarah said.

Reese looked at her, then at the food she'd barely touched. "Damn it, this was supposed to be a break for you. I'm sorry. You're not my counselor."

"No, but I think you need a friend. I'm happy to listen. It sounds like you have a lot you need to work out. I'm here for you."

"Thank you. So... what are your plans for the day?"

Sarah sighed and gestured at the laptop. "Same old, same old. Trying to keep the doors open."

"I wish there was something I could do to help."

"You're helping out enough, trust me. I'm grateful to have you here."

Reese said, "I just want to make myself useful."

"Be useful to yourself first. You need to think about what brought you here and what will get you home, where you belong."

"Yeah. I'm not sure that place exists anymore."

Sarah lifted a shoulder and waved a hand. "Then you need to figure that out so you can move on. Build a new life for yourself."

Reese's eyes burned with tears at the thought of such a monumental loss.

"Sorry. I didn't mean to sting you like that."

"No, it's just... it's tough love. It's the advice Winnie probably would have given me."

Sarah said, "Well, take all the time you need. I plan to take full advantage of having you available while you're around."

"Just point me where I can do the most good, boss."

They finished eating their breakfast in silence. Reese had no idea what steps she would have to take to get back to Coventry. Break up with Chloe? Formally apologize for the affair? Bathe naked in the ocean to cleanse herself before she was allowed back into the family home? She didn't know if any of that would work or if Winnie would accept them as appropriate penance. All she could do was work out how she felt about the situation, put herself on the path that felt right, and continue from there.

Winnie wasn't surprised to see her mother in the kitchen when she came downstairs, and she didn't try to hide the fact she hadn't been sleeping. She would never have been able to fool Ashlyn, anyway. Her hair was unwashed and she was wearing an oversized plaid shirt that hung on her like a dress. Since Reese's exile and May's disappearance, she'd stayed home. Will & Winn was shuttered along with Stormy Mouse with no clear indication of when they would reopen. Winnie couldn't bring herself to care much about the store. She assumed that was the reason for her mother's visit.

"Have you heard anything?" she asked as she went into the kitchen.

"No," Ashlyn said. "Are you taking care of yourself?"

Winnie opened a few cabinets in a show of looking for food she had no intention of eating. "Uh. Yeah. It's been a bit strange without the girls here. Quiet."

Ashlyn sat on a stool. "Grandy still isn't speaking. I just came from there."

Winnie dropped her hands to the countertop. The marble was cold against her fingertips, so she curled them up against her palm.

"Why would May do that?" she whispered, speaking as much to herself as to her mother. "What in the name of everything we believe in would make her use magic on a family member? On Grandy? She loves our grandmothers. She dotes on them. Cooks them dinner every night."

Ashlyn said, "Meemaw thinks she was lashing out because of the fight. She was stuck between her loyalty to you and to Cerys, so she snapped."

"If that was all it is, she would've come home by now."

"And Reese?"

"What about her?"

"Do you see yourself forgiving her?"

Winnie turned. "Do you see yourself forgiving Daddy?"

"That was a different situation."

"It was adultery. Reese did the same thing. It's the second time she's put her own carnal needs ahead of the family. A line had to be drawn."

Ashlyn said, "It's strange for you to accuse Reese of destroying the family when you're the one who sent both of your sisters away."

Winnie glared at her. "Are you saying this is my fault? I'm to blame for Reese sleeping with a married woman and May abusing her powers?"

"No. But your reaction to it may have been a bit overblown. Do you regret what you did? If taking it back meant Reese and May were both here right now..."

"Stop. Hypotheticals are stupid. What's done is done. I don't regret it. We have rules in this family."

"And one of those rules is that we have three Cabot girls to defend it. Fortunately there are three of us left. The two of us and Meemaw can work together until the twins show up again."

Winnie said, "That's not fair to you. It's especially not fair to Meemaw."

"So you're going to take it all on yourself?"

"No." She pinched the bridge of her nose. "I don't know what I'm going to do, Mommy." She surprised herself with that; she hadn't used 'mommy' since she was a toddler and now it was becoming a habit again. She decided to move on and hope her mother didn't latch onto it. "Protecting the island is our responsibility. Reese and May leaving is my fault. I'll figure out how to fix it."

Ashlyn looked skeptical. "I trust you. But first you need to fix yourself up. There's a meeting at the library. The whole town is coming."

"They wouldn't have something that big without warning."

"There was plenty of warning, two days ago. You would've heard if you bothered coming out of the house at any point since the girls left." She stood and stepped around the kitchen island. She put an arm around Winnie and guided her toward the stairs. "Now come on... if you insist on being this island's sole defender, you have to show up at the meeting. And you have to show up bathed and looking presentable. We have enough people calling us witches without you embracing the stereotype."

Winnie said, "I don't look that bad."

"You're a beautiful girl," Ashlyn said, responding without technically refuting the claim. "Go on upstairs. Take a bath. Put on some clean clothes. Do you have any clean clothes?" Winnie nodded. "I'll wait down here to take you to the meeting when you're presentable."

Winnie stopped at the base of the stairs. "Do you think there's a chance you would have forgiven Daddy if he came back?"

Ashley looked at the ground, then toward the window. She seemed to be doing anything she could not to meet her daughter's gaze.

"I don't know. But honey, Reese didn't betray *you*. She didn't make a vow to you. She's your sister, not your wife. The bond you two have runs a lot deeper. She's family. I think you can always find it in your heart to forgive family."

"I hope so." She kissed her mother on the cheek. "Thank you, Mom."

"Sure. Go on, hurry. The meeting is at lunchtime."

Winnie went upstairs. She paused at the door to May's room, looking in past the open curtain to Reese's bed. They both looked so utterly abandoned that it hurt to look at them for too long, but she forced herself to stay at the threshold. Their energy was fading. The beds had gone unslept in, the possessions were untouched, and soon she feared these would just be two ordinary rooms. She took a deep breath and rested her hand on the door frame.

She had no idea if she would be able to forgive Reese. She couldn't imagine laughing with her at the dinner table or snuggling with her on a snowy night without thinking she was an adulteress. She would never see her sister the same way again, a thought which prompted another: what if she literally never saw her sister again? Would she be able to bear it? And what sort of life would that be?

"I miss you," she said to the empty rooms. It was the one feeling she was positive about, and one she felt safe saying aloud.

CHAPTER SEVENTEEN

THE MEETING was held in the children's reading area of the library. The rows of wooden folding chairs were presided over by an enormous stuffed moose. Winnie sat beside her mother in the back row and tried not to make eye contact with anyone. She hadn't spoken to anyone on her staff since she closed the bakery without warning. She knew they had bills to pay, responsibilities that weren't being met because of her, and she couldn't bear to see their disappointment. Or worse, their pity. So instead she fiddled with the hem of her blouse and watched her shoes as the crowd filed in around her.

The island didn't have a mayor, but the town council took seats along the far wall under the alphabet chart. Normally Winnie would have been sitting near them with her sisters but it didn't feel right to take her usual place without Reese and May. She wondered, as she did hundreds of times a day, where they were. If they were safe. She knew Reese had left the island but no one had seen May since she left their grandmother.

A member of the council, a balding man named Troy Shelton, stood up and cleared his throat to silence the chatter. Winnie looked up and finally saw that Jessica Vaughn was in attendance. Not only that, the bitch had apparently been staring at her for quite a while. When she knew she'd been seen, Jessica smiled and arched an eyebrow. She winked.

The hairs on the back of Winnie's neck stood up. Her mother felt the change in her mood, looked at her, and then followed her line of sight.

"Is that her?"

Winnie nodded.

Troy Shelton gave command of the meeting to Lucas Passoth. Winnie could barely look him in the eye now that she knew what Reese had been up to with his wife. He smiled at the crowd.

"I want to thank everyone for coming out this afternoon. We've been working for a while on something big that's going to benefit the whole town, and the time has come for us to reveal our plans. I'd like to bring up Miss Jessica Vaughn of GreenVault Development. Miss Vaughn was originally born on Coventry Island and she hopes to use the things she's learned on the mainland to benefit her hometown. Miss Vaughn?"

She smoothed her hands over her skirt and smiled as she stood up. "Please, it's Jessica. Thank you, Lucas." She took his place at the front of the room. "It's interesting to be up here. I first read *A Light in the Attic* right over there on some beanbag chairs. I see a lot of familiar faces here, too." She scanned the crowd and let her gaze linger on Winnie.

"As Lucas said, I work for a company called GreenVault Development. What we do is go around and look for places that can benefit from a fresh coat of paint and some new blood. When my bosses asked me if I knew of any potential sites that needed new life, I thought of my old hometown. I know what a lot of you are thinking. You hear the word 'change' and it scares you. But I'm not here to bulldoze the place you love and replace it with a Wal-Mart. That's not what's happening here. All I want to do is put some wind into your sails."

Winnie's hands were balled into fists. Her mother reached over and touched her hand, but it did nothing to soothe the rage swirling in her mind.

"We're talking about a hotel so visitors can stay overnight. Visitors staying longer means more money flowing into local businesses. It means more jobs for your kids so they don't have to go off-island like I did. We're talking about a few condos on the northern shore that might draw a few celebrities to call Coventry their home. I hear Charlize Theron is looking for a place in the Pacific Northwest. Who wouldn't want Furiosa as a neighbor? As long as she stays off the roads, of course."

The crowd chuckled.

"The town is not forcing this on you, of course," Jessica said. "You have a voice. We're going to have a vote next week where you can decide for yourselves. But I want you to think long and hard about what a 'yes' vote means. This is a beautiful town, but it's just not self-sustainable. The tourists may come and they may not, and a slow year means everyone suffers. My company is offering an end to slow years once and for all."

"Liar," Winnie said.

Jessica looked at her, and every head swiveled to face her. "Oh. Hello, Arwyn. Could your sisters not make it to the meeting?"

Winnie stood up. Ashlyn grabbed her hand, acting as an anchor. "You're lying to these people."

"No," Jessica said, tilting her head slightly. "I'm telling them our plans. My company wants to hire a construction crew to build a hotel near the docks, condos along the shoreline, and homes on the north shore. That's what will be on the ballot and that is what we intend to do. No more, no less."

"You want to build a hotel which will block views of the water. It would disrupt the natural flow between land and water. It would devastate the island's energy. You want to build condos along the shoreline where rich outsiders can benefit from the best views while we're stuck in increasingly neglected parts of the town. You want playhouses for the rich and famous, which will be flypaper for their entourage and paparazzi. The island we know, our home, will effectively cease to exist."

Jessica said, "That's all very doom and gloom, Winnie, but my company has a sterling reputation. The newspaper is going to carry a full article about us so everyone will be fully informed about who we are. You'll all be able to see for yourselves just how respected we are in the industry. I know I wouldn't want some stranger barging in and changing everything, but Coventry is my home, too. No matter how long I might have been away from it."

Winnie started gathering energy in her palms, unaware she was doing it until she felt her mother drawing it away from her. She looked down and saw her mother staring up at her with anger and disappointment in her eyes. If Reese and May had been there she could have kept her cool. She would never have interrupted the meeting in the first place because she would have been balanced by their presence. She suddenly realized she hadn't been without them since she was six.

The entire room was watching her. Jessica had folded her hands behind her back, apparently waiting to see what would happen next. And of course, Winnie realized, this had been her plan all along. Revealing Reese's sin a few days before the meeting so the family would have time to collapse before she made her true plans known. The pictures weren't the endgame. The pictures were just a way to ensure her enemies were rocked back on their heels.

"Were you done?" Jessica finally asked.

A few people in the crowd chuckled. Winnie's face burned, and she pulled her hand away from her mother's.

"You still have to get the vote," she said. "Coventry Island won't be complicit in its own destruction."

"This isn't about destruction, Miss Cabot," Troy Shelton interjected. "This is just another evolution of the island, you see. Was Squire's Isle destroyed when they built the airport? Was it destroyed when they established their radio station? No! They're growing stronger every year! Meanwhile, we're lingering in the last century. We barely even have wifi or cell service here."

Jessica said, "Ah, another thing we'll be addressing as quickly as possible. The internet is coming to Coventry Island!"

The crowd murmured excitedly and Winnie was suddenly terrified the vote would pass. "This island..." she said. "This island isn't... it's..."

"This island isn't one family." Winnie didn't know if she said it as angrily as it sounded, but she still hunched her shoulders as if attacked. "It's not three sisters. Or, I suppose more accurately, one woman. If you don't like what I'm proposing, you're free to vote no. But the people who want to see this island take a step forward into the future? They can vote yes. And I sincerely hope they do."

Troy Shelton stood back up, hoping to put an end to the argument. "Miss Vaughn has agreed to stay at the library for the rest of the afternoon answering any questions people might have about her company or their plans for the island. Thank you to everyone for coming out and we hope you all show up again next Tuesday for the big vote!"

Winnie turned and rushed for the door before most of the room had risen from their seats. She was trembling with anger, both at what had just happened and how she allowed herself to be played. She'd let Jessica turn her into a weapon against her sisters and she'd gone off just as expected. She could only hope there was time to find them and make amends before the vote. She couldn't stop Jessica by herself but maybe with their help she could work out a plan.

She was almost to the door when someone touched her shoulder. She turned and saw Lucas smiling down at her, mere inches away. The word *affair* blasted to the front of her mind and she jumped back as if she could keep it from slipping out of her mouth. The reaction caused her to smack into the door, her head bouncing off the metal edge. Lucas flinched at the sight and reached out again, this time as if he wanted to cover the wound. Luckily he stopped short of actually touching her.

"I'm so sorry I startled you. Are you okay? That had to sting."

"I'm fine." She touched the wound and hissed. There was a smear of blood on her fingers when she looked at them, but she hid that from Lucas. "I just... it was a lot to take in. The meeting."

He nodded. "I know. Exciting, isn't it?"

She refused to comment, instead applying pressure to her wound. It was throbbing now. She looked past Lucas and saw her mother watching them.

"I feel like this is the finish line to all my hard work. Of course, I know there's still a lot of work to be done, but I've kept this island rolling for a very long time. I just wanted what was best for the island, and GreenVault is going to be a huge help with that goal." He hesitated. "But actually, I was trying to catch you to talk about something else. The past few days, Will & Winn has been closed every time I go by. Is everything okay? If you need something or if it's a cashflow issue, I'm sure we can look at some credit options..."

"No. No, there's no... uh, I've been sick..."

Lucas' face fell into something uncomfortably close to pity. "Oh, I'm sorry to hear that. Is there anything I can do? If you need to see a doctor, I know a guy on the mainland. He's great."

"I'll be... I'm fine."

"Are you sure?"

She started to back out of the room. "Yes. Sorry. I have to go."

Lucas didn't move to stop her. "Okay. I hope we can count on your vote next week! The town has been surviving for a long time, and GreenVault is going to help it thrive!"

Winnie ignored the obvious campaign slogan and ran from the building. She needed to get home. She needed Reese's things, May's things, and then she could pinpoint them no matter how far away they might have wandered. Once she knew where they were, she could bring them back. If that meant throwing herself on Reese's mercy to get forgiveness, then she would do that. The island's future was at stake, and it was her fault. She'd fallen for Jessica's ruse, been a victim to her machinations just as Reese had been when they were teenagers.

Jessica had almost defeated the Cabot sisters once, but this time she was going after the whole island and she'd used Winnie as a tool. She would not abide that, even if she had to stand against Jessica Vaughn and GreenVault all by herself.

CHAPTER EIGHTEEN

THERE WAS a baseball field a few blocks from the women's shelter with a long stretch of concrete steps along one side which served as bleachers. Sarah liked to take her lunch there if things weren't too busy. It let her see most of the town, and she could still see the shelter, but it was far enough away that she didn't feel caught up in its orbit. On the third day Reese was at the shelter, Sarah invited her along as a thank-you for bringing her breakfast.

"I didn't bring my own lunch."

"I packed for two."

Reese said, "You did? Why?"

"Because I wanted to ask you along yesterday, but I didn't have enough to share. Come on."

It was obvious that the bleachers were a special, solitary place for Sarah, and Reese appreciated how much it meant to be invited along. She followed Sarah across the field, past the empty dugout and concession stand. Sarah climbed to the top step and sat facing the field, and Reese sat one step below her. On the other side of the far fence they could see sunlight glinting off the Strait. It made that part of town look like it was glowing. Sarah opened her lunch bag and handed Reese a sandwich.

"Is tuna okay?"

"Free food means no preference. Tuna's fine."

Sarah smiled and used her lap as a plate. Reese unwrapped her sandwich and opened her chips. The meal was a simple one, but comforting. It reminded her of being in school, or of mealtime with her sisters. There was no need for them to break the silence with small talk. They ate in silence for a while, only the crunch of chips and the crinkle of plastic between them.

"Can..." She coughed to clear her throat of an errant crumb. Sarah passed her a milk carton, and Reese thanked her after taking a sip. "You really think of everything."

"Be prepared."

"So, what I was going to say... can I ask what brought you to the shelter? If it's too personal, I understand."

Sarah said, "It's fine. There's no big story. I wasn't abused, I didn't escape a horrible relationship. I just watched the news too many times and saw the same thing over and over. I found out the shelter existed, but it wasn't really doing anything because no one was willing to do the work. So I decided to give up my dream of being a concert pianist and took the online classes I needed to get qualified."

Reese looked at Sarah's long, slender fingers. "You wanted to be a pianist?"

"Yep. I would've had a good chance if I ever learned how to play." Reese laughed. "I just liked the idea of sitting up on stage in a tuxedo wiggling my fingers while people applauded."

Reese raised an eyebrow. "How old were you when you came up with that fantasy...?"

Sarah smirked. "Twelve. And yeah, Freud. I put the pieces together, too. Dressing in a suit, working my fingers to the delight of a crowd. The only thing missing was the other woman."

They lapsed back into silence until Sarah cleared her throat.

"So... in my line of work, you learn not to ask for stories. The reason people come to the shelter is their own business and they don't have to share if they don't want to. But I've also learned when someone *wants* to tell the story but doesn't know how to break the ice. The way you talk about your sisters and the way you look at the other women in the shelter... I can tell you miss them. The bond you have must be very strong. If you want to talk about what happened, I'm here to listen."

Reese picked at the crust of her sandwich. The humor from a moment ago had evaporated. "It's kind of a long story."

"We have time."

"We really are close. We always have been. My twin sister and I have shared a room our whole lives. When we were teenagers, there was… there was a woman. Jessica. May had a crush on her. She was obsessed, but she never told me or Winnie because she wasn't comfortable with her sexuality yet. So she followed Jessica around like a puppy. Jessica eventually got tired of it and decided to be cruel. It was a small town. She knew May had a twin sister. So she found me. Flirted with me. And Jessica was gorgeous, I was a horny teenager, and I thought she was interested in me.

"We started hanging out. I kept it secret for the same reason May did. One day she asked if she could come back to my house. Winnie was at work, and May was supposed to be with our grandparents. So… empty house, hot girl asking to see my bedroom. It's a no-brainer, right?"

Sarah shrugged. "It was when I was a teenager."

Reese nodded and squinted toward the sunny water. "We were on the bed. Things were progressing. I'm not trying to be prurient or anything, with the details. It's just that the timeline is important."

"I understand."

"So we were on the bed. Her shirt is unbuttoned and I'm seeing a real girl in a bra for the first time. Her hand is on my leg. And I'm wearing a skirt, so it's skin on skin. We're kissing. We're touching. And then out of nowhere she pulls back and says 'Your sister has a crush on me.' I thought she meant Winnie because they're closer in age. But she said May. And then she said, 'Do you think we should stop?'"

Sarah grunted and put her hand against her forehead. "That's diabolical. I'm assuming you told her to keep going."

"Uh, in a way. I moved her hand higher on my leg."

"Sure."

"So we took off more of our clothes. Things started to happen. And in the middle of it, May walked in."

Sarah said, "So she saw you…"

"Mm-hmm. With the woman she was madly in love with. Well, teenage-love."

"She must have been heartbroken."

Reese said, "I've never seen anyone look so betrayed. That was even before she found out I knew how she felt and kept going."

"How did she find out?"

"Jessica told her."

"The bitch!"

Reese laughed quietly. "Yeah... it took a lot of time for us to get back to normal after that. If it hadn't been for Winnie mediating the whole thing, we might never have reconciled. We talked. We figured out Jessica had been playing me from the moment we met, and May realized I was as much a victim as she was. So May, Winnie, and I joined forces to kick Jessica off the island."

"How did you do that?"

"Oh. Uh, magic."

Sarah laughed.

"No, I'm serious. The island is special. It has energies. We can tap into those energies for spells and blessings. We're witches."

"I know witches," Sarah said. "They don't really do magic spells over a cauldron or ride broomsticks."

Reese said, "We don't do that stuff, either. And we're not Wiccan. That's something else entirely. But we have similar ties to nature and the energy in everything." She looked around and put her sandwich down. "See the apple tree over there?"

Sarah looked, nodded.

Reese brushed the crumbs from her hands. She scooted to the edge of the stone step and focused on the tree. She held out one hand with her fingers flat.

"Are you going to juggle some apples in the air?"

Reese ignored her. She could probably have done something like that, but she was planning a more impressive feat. She closed her eyes and slowly spread her fingers. She pictured the tree in her mind and 'read' what signals it was sending out. It was strong and spry, full of life. She pressed her lips together and tilted her head to the side like she was reading the spines of books in the library. She felt the life inside the trees and narrowed her attention to one small piece of it.

"Is it supposed to be visible, or...?"

"It's harder when I'm not on the island," Reese said quickly so it wouldn't ruin her concentration. "Almost."

She heard Sarah chuckle quietly. She didn't let it get to her.

An apple dropped from the tree and thudded onto the ground. Sarah stopped laughing, startled, but the real trick was still to come. A squirrel dropped out of the branches and clung to the trunk, head pointed to the ground and his tail twitching like an antenna. He hesitated.

"C'mon, buddy," Reese whispered. "You promised."

He spiraled down the trunk, paused again on a root, and then picked up the fallen apple. He grabbed it with his forepaws and, in an awkward shuffle, ran over to the stone steps. Sarah tensed and pulled her feet back, twisting away as he approached, but Reese just smiled. The squirrel dropped the apple and Reese dropped her hand to deliver the reward: the remains of her bag of potato chips. The squirrel grabbed it, held it in its mouth, and fled with its treasure.

Sarah said, "What the hell just happened?"

"We made a trade. There were a couple of squirrels in the tree, but he was the one who wanted some chips. So I agreed to swap."

"No, you... you just gave a squirrel a bag of chips because he brought you an apple."

Reese said, "The bag will get thrown away. I told him that when he's done, the Shiny goes into Big Green. He understands, but he also knows a Steller's Jay who might want it for her nest. They like shiny things."

Sarah said, "*Wait.* Wait a second. You just had a conversation with a *squirrel?*"

"Not really. We just conversed."

"That's *insane.*"

Reese said, "You just saw it."

"I... I guess I did." She dropped her hands and stared at Reese. "I'm sorry. I just have trouble believing this is possible. What else can you do?"

"Since I've been at the shelter, I've been cleansing the public spaces. I put blessings on the donated clothes, and I help ease the minds of women who come to you for help."

Sarah chuckled softly. "I'll be damned. I thought there was something in the air. It felt like... like the first days of Spring, when everything is fresh and renewed. I thought it was just global warming."

Reese smiled. "I want to do everything I can to help."

"It shows. I'm just glad that now I know who to thank." She cleared her throat. "So, uh, beyond the magic thing, I assume your current exile doesn't have anything to do with what happened back then."

"Sort of. The past few months, I've been sleeping with a woman in town. She happens to be married. And her husband funds a lot of business on the island, including Winnie's bakery. Jessica came back and somehow had pictures that proved we were having an affair. If her husband finds out, he could destroy

Winnie's work. Winnie blew up at me, rightly so, and kicked me out for not only threatening her business but breaking our family's number one sin. Oh... Daddy had an affair. I left that part out. So we've always considered that the most unforgiveable thing anyone could do."

Sarah whistled through her teeth. "That's a lot to take in. How did your twin take the affair?"

Reese wiggled her hand. "She sided with Winnie. She sort of had to, or she would've been kicked out along with me. She let me know that she doesn't hate me, so that's something." She looked down at her shoes and blinked away tears. "So how can I go back? I was in the wrong. I put Winnie's livelihood at risk. I lied to her and May both."

"You screwed up, big time. And you pissed your sister off. I don't have sisters, but that seems like par for the course when it comes to siblings. You know what else siblings do to each other? They forgive. They might be mad for a while. Winnie might lose her job. But at the end of the day, you can count on one another. She's not going to cut you out forever."

Reese said, "You didn't see how mad she got."

Sarah moved down so she was sitting beside Reese on the same step. "The thing that happened when you were teenagers. You were tongue-deep in the naughty bits of the woman your sister was in love with. She walked in and caught you. In my mind, that's pretty damn unforgiveable. But she did. She remembered she loved you more than anything, and she found it in her heart to accept your apology. You just have to give Winnie the chance to do the same thing. Your life isn't over. Your life is changing."

"I don't want it to change."

"Of course you don't!" Sarah said, laughing. "But that doesn't stop it from changing. Life just keeps rolling and all you can do is control the steering. So... life is rolling. Where are you going to steer?"

"I don't know."

"Good. I'd be worried if you thought you immediately knew the answer to that question." She reached out and patted Reese's knee. "Keep thinking about it. Until you figure it out, the shelter is happy to have you."

"Thanks, Sarah."

"Sure. And in the meantime, judging from what you've told me about your family, I bet you're used to home-cooked meals. I can't promise it'll be as good as what your sister can whip up, but if you wanted to come over some night, I can cook you something better than what you'll get at the shelter."

Reese said, "I... think that would be nice. It'll be nice to get out of the shelter a little. See the town."

"Yeah. We'll find a time that works for both of us." She looked toward the tree. "Could you teach me that thing with the squirrel?"

Reese smiled. "No. Sorry. It's not exactly a... a teachable thing."

"I understand. I just thought it would be nice to tell the assholes to leave my birdfeeder alone."

Reese laughed and settled back to finish eating her sandwich. A few more days spending time with Sarah and the other ladies at the shelter didn't sound all that bad to her. She could figure out a longer-term plan another day.

CHAPTER NINETEEN

MAY WOKE on the fourth day and rolled onto her side to watch the sunrise through the trees. She was naked on the front porch of a cabin, her clothes drying on a line that stretched from one support beam to a nearby tree. Her feet were sore but no longer throbbing. She sat up, laced her fingers, and stretched her arms above her head. She grunted as her back popped, twisting one way and then the other. She dropped her arms into her lap and blinked out at the world.

She only had a vague idea of how long she'd been away from home. Four or five long days. Almost a week in which Winnie and Reese continued their lives without her. Or maybe they were frantically searching for her. She hadn't seen any boats, and she stayed fairly close to the shore when she walked. It was the easiest way to prevent herself from getting lost. Sometimes she wandered deeper into the woods or climbed a rock face to see how far she could see from the top.

She'd been worried about food when she first set out, but the island provided. There were unlocked cabins here and there with non-perishable items in their cupboards. She had come across farmhouses whose owners were more than happy to provide her with more food than she asked for. Full meals rather than the biscuits she'd asked for, with tall glasses of ice tea or milk. The people of the island are so kind. So generous with what they have.

May stood and walked to the clothes she left fluttering in the breeze. They were dry but she didn't put them on. She enjoyed the way the morning breeze was touching her skin, caressing her shoulders and hair in a very pleasant way, and she didn't want clothes to impede that. She did put on her socks and shoes on since she planned to go down to the shore where it was rocky and she didn't want to cut her feet.

The past few days, she hadn't wasted mental energy on things like direction or destination. She was too busy thinking about her grandmother and everything she'd done to them. The lies and deceit. The worst moment in her life was orchestrated by the woman she thought loved her more than anything. She thought of the countless nights she'd spent making her grandmothers dinner. The conversation and the jokes. The routine they built for themselves with crosswords and game shows. Through it all, Grandy had been conspiring against her. Jessica Vaughn was just a tool, a weapon, wielded against her granddaughters.

And the weapon had just been deployed again. Reese. She was so disappointed in Reese, but she was also disappointed in how Winnie handled it. Anger and exile. Those weren't Cabot traits. They were a singular force standing together against the world. But Grandy proved that wasn't true, hadn't she? If she could turn against the family then maybe Winnie was just taking after their elders.

Something moved in the trees to the west. It was a sudden sound that ended too quickly to be natural, and May stopped walking to listen. She'd heard similar noises the past few days and no longer worried it was someone trying to sneak up on her. If it was an actual person it would require inhuman abilities of stealth and patience. But she couldn't shake the feeling that she was being observed. She closed her eyes and tried to hear the sound again. Maybe if she could pinpoint it, she could spot something to explain it.

But the sound didn't come again. She slumped her shoulders in disappointment and continued on.

She did wonder about Grandy and Meemaw. How were they coping with the curse? Did Meemaw know the whole story? She should have stayed long enough to see how deeply the betrayal ran, but she couldn't spend another minute in that house. For now she could simply believe that Meemaw was innocent. The truth would come out in due course, and she had enough to occupy her mind without losing both her grandmothers in one fell swoop.

When she reached the shore, she stood in the cover of trees long enough to determine there were no boats close enough to observe her. She was in a tear-drop shaped cove which was mostly enclosed on both sides by long, narrow spits of land. The only part of the Strait with a clear view of where she was standing was completely empty. She stepped out and cautiously made her way across the shore where the waves lapped against the shore. She crouched, knees to her chest, and cupped her hands in the water.

"Thank you," she said to the island, "for this beauty and wonder. Thank you for allowing me to stand here and witness your beauty."

"You're welcome."

May was surprised but unafraid. She twisted at the waist and looked behind her. Standing on the shore between her and the point where she'd exited the trees was a woman. She was gorgeous, with brown skin and a wide spray of curly black hair that exploded from her head and cascaded down her back. She was completely nude, her full breasts capped with dark nipples, and her mound hidden by a patch of soft hair.

"Hello," May said.

The woman grinned. "Good morning, Maeve Wren."

May crossed her arms over her chest and twisted so the woman was seeing her from the side. "You know my name?"

"Yes. Just as you know mine."

"You've been following me."

The woman stepped closer. "You've been tracing my lines."

May tilted her head to the side. There was something about this woman, something unnatural. No. Something *too* natural.

"You're..." Her eyes skipped from the woman to the island behind her.

She smiled and dipped her head. "Yes."

"What's your name?"

"When I was first given a name it was N'scha'cha Twh."

May said, "N'scha..."

"You may call me Nish."

"Thank you." May realized she had lowered her hands. It seemed ridiculous to cover herself up again, especially since Nish was also naked, but she was uncertain about what to do with her arms once she was aware of them again. "Are you real?"

Nish moved her eyes past May, just over her right shoulder, as she considered her response. "You've felt the island in your soul. You've spoken to it and heard its reply. I give the question back to you: am I real?"

"Yes," May said without hesitation.

"As for why I've been following you... I've felt the Cabot family in my bones since the first of your kind set foot on my shores. Did you think I wouldn't feel when you shattered. I knew where I could find Arwyn Mavis, and the soul of Cerys Aveline has always been too tormented for me. But you, Maeve Wren..." She had come closer without May realizing it, now close enough to reach out and cup May's cheek. May closed her eyes and turned her head into the caress. "I missed your voice most of all."

The touch on her cheek felt like the wind, but there was a consciousness there. A warmth. With her eyes closed her mind forgot that there was a person standing in front of her.

"You've almost arrived home, Maeve Wren. You walked my borders nearly in their entirety. What will you do next?"

"I don't know. My family... my family." She shook her head. "I don't know if I can trust them."

"They're the only ones you can trust," Nish said. "Just as it always has been. There have always been Cabot girls on the island, and they have always protected me. They've watched over me until their time is done."

May opened her eyes. She was alone in water that reached to her thighs. She realized she was ruining her shoes and socks, but she didn't care. She realized what the island was trying to tell her and smiled. She turned her face to the sky and held her arms out to her sides, palms flat.

"Thank you, N'scha'cha Twh! I use your proper name to show respect and gratitude for what you have shown me, for the truth you shone into my eyes like a ray of the sun. Thank you."

A wave gently impacted the back of her thighs and she gasped when it splashed between her legs. She started for shore but then remembered how Nish's hand on her cheek felt like wind. Could the water have just been a different kind of touch...? She tucked her hair behind her ears and searched the shore for any indication N'scha'cha Twh was still watching, but she was alone. There was a slanted stone nearby and, after a moment to consider what she was about to do, she walked to it and lay down with her legs mostly submerged.

"N'scha'cha Twh," she whispered as she stretched out on the

stone. She made the last sound a soft exhale, using the tip of her tongue to push the consonants out between her teeth. May put her arms out to the side and let her hands dip into the water. She brought them up and let the water pour over her breasts. The cold water tightened her nipples and spread gooseflesh across her chest. She squirmed and moved her feet apart.

The rhythm of the water seemed to change. The water pressed between her legs, retreated, and then pressed back with almost conscious effort. May bit her bottom lip and cupped her breasts. She arched her back. With her eyes closed she could picture N'scha'cha Twh on top of her. Hands which didn't exist explored her body and ran down her stomach. She drew in a breath as fingers with skin as soft as water caressed her.

"N'scha'cha Twh," May said again, then swallowed against the lump in her throat.

This wasn't masturbation. This was sex, the closest to sex she'd ever come, and it allowed her to put herself in Reese's shoes. It didn't excuse adultery or the original betrayal but it helped her understand it in a way she never had before. Jessica, desirable and eager, would have been nearly impossible to resist. May suddenly realized that she *had* to catch them in the midst of it for the betrayal to be complete. If she hadn't, Reese, probably would have confessed and May's pain would have been much diminished.

Nish pressed against her again using the water and May writhed, reaching out for her lover but finding only air and water.

"Please, N'scha'cha Twh," the name rolled off her tongue now, as natural as her own or the names of her sisters.

"Your pleasure is mine," the wind said.

May put a hand up where she assumed the other woman's face would be. The waves pushed higher on her body and slid down over her breasts, her stomach, down her legs. Another wave and this time her hair got wet. She laughed and dropped her hands to her sides as the water continued to crash against her. Her legs closed when she came, her stomach convulsing and her toes curling at the sensation. The water dragged across her body. It seemed to pool over her lap, swirling in the space between her thighs, and she could almost imagine a tongue swirling over her clit.

"Thank you," she gasped. She opened her eyes and stared at the island as she caught her breath. The trees swayed in the same breeze that blew across her nipples. Her entire body felt refreshed by what had happened and, though she wasn't exactly sure about the details, she knew that from now on she would feel like a liar if she described herself as a virgin. She just hoped no one asked after the identity of her partner.

She sat up, her hair wet, and put a hand between her legs. She still felt sensitive there, though not sore or in pain. The loss of her virginity had been tender and comfortable in every way possible. Her legs were still in the water. It was only a matter of time before a boat passed by or someone hiked through the clearing and saw her. Frankly she couldn't have cared less. She had legs and a stomach and breasts with nipples. Who cared if someone saw her naked? It was just a body. One of billions on the planet. She dragged her fingers up her sides and shivered.

"You know what you have to do," N'scha'cha Twh whispered on the breeze, and May finally recognized the voice as one she'd heard her entire life. Did that mean it was just a manifestation of her own internal monologue or had the island been whispering to her since she was a girl? It didn't matter. She stood and walked through the water back to shore. Before she returned to land, she crouched down and scooped a few handfuls of water over the top of her head and let it cascade down her back.

May walked back to the cabin and retrieved her clothes. She dressed and looked to the west. Town was just about a mile away, if she didn't meander, and she didn't intend to waste any more time. She left to be alone with her thoughts and figure out what to do. She'd succeeded at that.

It was time to go home.

CHAPTER TWENTY

AFTER LUNCH, Reese went directly back to her room to pack. Technically she was unpacking. Most of the clothes she'd been wearing belonged to the shelter, and she put everything aside so she could start a load of laundry before she left. She didn't plan to leave with anything more than she'd arrived with. She was almost finished making the bed when Sarah knocked on the door.

"Reese, I was wondering... oh. You're leaving."

"I think so." Reese smoothed down the last corner of the sheet and turned to see Sarah looked upset. "I know I'm sort of leaving you in the lurch here, but you made me realize I can't solve my problems this far from home. I need to go back and face the mess I made, no matter how much it hurts."

Sarah said, "Absolutely. No, I absolutely agree with that. But I guess that means the dinner I promised you will have to wait."

"Probably. Sorry."

"It's fine." After a moment, she sighed and tilted her head to the side. "No, you know, it's not fine. Sorry. I just convinced you that talking things out was the smart thing to do, and now I'm clamming up. I'm sad you're leaving, Reese. I wish you would have come over tonight so I could cook dinner for you, and put on music for you, and show you what I'm like when I'm not stressing over a hundred budget things. I wanted to find out if you would be attracted to me if you saw me like that."

Reese stared. "Oh. I mean... I probably would be."

"Yeah?"

"Well, I'm attracted to this version of you. So that other one sounds... pretty good."

Sarah smiled and looked away. "Oh."

"But the thing on the island... with the married woman. That's technically still going on. Even though I think I saw her true colors back when this all blew up. Or maybe I didn't. I don't know." She rubbed her forehead. "The point is that I don't know what's happening with Chloe, and I really don't want to muddy up anything with you by starting it too early."

"That's probably the smart thing to do."

Reese sighed. "I really wish I was dumb."

Sarah laughed. "You and me both." She came into the room. "Coventry Island isn't that far away from here. Maybe I'll take a long weekend. You can show me the sights."

"It's a small island. Unless you want to go whale-watching, there aren't many sights."

"I'm sure I can find something to look at."

Reese blushed and tucked her hair behind her ears. "Okay. I should probably get going."

"Do you need a ride?"

"Um. Yeah, if you have time. I was just going to walk to the bus station."

Sarah shook her head and waved for Reese to follow her. "Come on. I'll let Irene know I'll be out for an hour or so." They went toward the kitchen. "Have you thought about what you're going to say when you get there?"

"No. But it's my sisters. I figure whatever I need to say will come out when I get there. That's usually how it works with Winnie and May."

"Are they... you know... like you?"

"More powerful than me," Reese said. "Winnie has so much strength it's scary sometimes. I think she holds back so no one will be afraid of her. And May... I can feel the power in her. It's the twin thing. She's more powerful than any of us but I don't think she even realizes it."

Sarah said, "I bet they say the same thing about you."

Reese almost denied it, but they probably did. May was always asking her to lead them in mediation and the blessings.

"The three of you together must be something to see."

"Yeah," Reese said. "We can move mountains when we put our minds to it."

Winnie sat in front of the altar, hands balled into fists on her thighs. Her head was down, voice trembling with unshed tears. She wouldn't cry. Crying would be to admit defeat. The candles were burning and she'd said the prayers, but nothing felt right. She'd spent too long neglecting it. The rituals were stagnant and it was all her fault. The island would fall, her sisters would crumble, and it would all be her fault. She opened her eyes and blinked away the moisture, held her hands out, and unfolded her fingers.

"Mother of all, we praise you. Blessings to you and to us..." Her voice cracked. She folded her hands back into fists. "Please..."

"You're doing the wrong one."

Winnie jumped and twisted at the waist. May was standing in the doorway of the bedroom. She was tanned and her hair looked wet but unwashed, her clothes filthy. She was carrying her shoes in her hand, and her feet were scratched and muddy between the toes. But she smiled sheepishly and suddenly she was the most radiant thing Winnie had ever seen.

"Maeve." She got up, her legs protesting after being folded so long, and fell into her sister's arms. May caught her easily and kissed her cheeks and eyelids. Winnie finally let out a short, desperate sob. It was easier to give in with someone there to protect her. "I thought I'd lost you forever. I'm so sorry. If you want to kick me out so Cerys can come back, I'll understand. I was wrong."

"Arwyn, sh. No one is getting kicked out. You exiled Cerys and I abandoned you and we all isolated ourselves, and that was very wrong. That made us weak. But we need to be strong, Arwyn. Can you do that for me?"

Winnie furrowed her brow. "I'm the older sister here. I'm supposed to be the voice of reason."

"When you've stopped throwing hissy fits, then you can be in charge again. For now, it's my turn. I did a lot of thinking while I was gone, and I know what we have to do."

"Get Reese back."

May nodded. "Yes, that's part of it. But first we need to fix what you let crumble. We need to build up our energy again."

"I've been trying!" She turned and gestured at the altar. "It's not working."

"Like I said when I came in, you're doing the wrong one.

Come on." She took Winnie's hand. They went back to the altar and knelt beside each other, backs straight. "Light the candles again."

Winnie picked up the matches and struck them, carefully placing the flame against each wick. She settled back and looked at May for guidance.

May took Winnie's hand in hers. "Oh great goddess, we ask for your healing. The hands of Hygieia on our weary brow guided by the wisdom of Brigid, heal the wounds we've allowed to form in the body of our family. Use the mercy of Guanyin to forgive us for these self-inflicted wounds. Let the bonds become even stronger as they heal."

Winnie gasped as she felt the prayer beginning to work. It was like waking up healthy for the first time after a lingering illness. She could breathe and feel her own soul again. She squeeze May's hand and felt her grip tighten in response. She wet her lips and began to speak the recitation of the prayer in harmony with her little sister.

"What's that?"

Reese looked away from the window, snapped out of her trance by Sarah's question. "Hm? What's what?"

"You were muttering something."

"Was I...?"

Reese tried to remember. She looked down at her hands, resting in her lap, and realized the fingers were curled as if she was holding something. She felt calmer than she had since leaving the island. Or, really, since the night Winnie confronted her with the truth. Something was different. Something was happening on the island and, even though she was still miles away, she could feel it working on the dark and sorrow in her chest.

"I don't know," she said. "It's nothing..."

Sarah smiled knowingly. "Witch sister stuff?"

Reese nodded. She normally hated when anyone outside the family used the word witch, but something about the way Sarah used it made it okay. "Yeah."

"Don't let me interrupt if you have to keep going."

They rode in silence, but eventually Reese closed her eyes and leaned back against the headrest.

"Oh great goddess," she whispered under her breath, "we ask for your healing..."

After they recited the prayer three times - one for each of them - May went to take a long bath. Winnie was as refreshed as if she'd slept for a week. Her mind was clear and she was brimming with energy. She gathered May's clothes and took them to the laundry room, treating the mud and grass stains before they had a chance to set in. There were a few rips and tears, but nothing an hour with needle and thread couldn't cure.

Once the clothes were dealt with, she took a sandwich and a container of DuChilly nuts upstairs. She knocked on the bathroom door and May invited her inside.

May was reclining in the tub, a washcloth draped across her chest and her arms hanging over the edge. She opened her eyes to smile at Winnie, but the smile widened when she saw what she was bringing.

"DuChilly. Is it my birthday?"

"No, but you are a princess." She sat on the floor. May took the nuts, screwing up her face as she wrestled with the lid. Winnie smiled at the spectacle and rested her head on the side of the tub. She slipped her hand under May's and brought it to her lips so she could kiss the fingers. "I missed you so much, May."

"I know. I'm sorry I left the way I did. But it was necessary to clear my head."

"Was it also necessary to take away Grandy's voice?"

A cloud passed over May's face. She looked away, toward the window but not at it. "Do you think I would have done something like that on a whim?"

"No," Winnie said. "But I can't imagine a reason big enough to justify it."

"Be glad you can't." She took in a breath through her nose and let it out slowly. "Have you seen Reese? She was supposed to be staying at the Stormy Mouse. It's time for her to come home."

Winnie hunched her shoulders, dreading this admission. "No, she's... she's not there. She left. She left the island the same day you disappeared."

May sat up sharply, the towel falling away just enough to reveal the side of her bare breast. Winnie was shocked to see so much of her sister, but she was more concerned with the fear in her eyes.

"Reese has been off the island? That's not good, Arwyn."

"I know, but I thought... I didn't think it was wise to chase her even when I realized I was wrong. And May, I was so wrong. I know what Jessica is trying to do to the island."

May said, "You'll have to tell me on the move." She groped for a larger towel. Winnie picked it up, held it open for her, and May stood up and let herself be wrapped in it. "We have to find Reese and bring her back. The three of us need to be together again."

"I couldn't agree more. But Maeve, where would we even begin looking?"

"She's my other half," May said. "I'll know where to find her. Come on... we have to hurry."

May went into her bedroom leaving Winnie pacing in the hall as she changed. She didn't take long, grabbing the first blouse and pair of jeans from her closet and tugging them on over a clean pair of underwear. As they left the house, May reached back and grabbed Winnie's hand. Winnie grabbed back with the other hand, hanging onto May as if she was being dragged across the lawn. The depression and defeat that had been closing around her throat like a choker was now a distant memory. She watched May's hair, still wet from the bath, as it streamed behind her.

It occurred to her, in a very vague sense, that she was letting her baby sister take charge. She was happy to do it, though. She hadn't been feeling very much like an older sister or a leader. May certainly seemed to have a handle on the situation, so Winnie was more than willing to be a follower.

May took Winnie out of their neighborhood, down a side street, and down toward the dock. She was going so fast that it was hard for Winnie to keep up. May was younger but she'd always been the tallest of the sisters, and Winnie almost tripped over her feet a few times before she finally released May's hand to run at her own pace.

Barty had just arrived at the dock, the wake still swirling behind his boat. Winnie said, "Are we going to the mainland?"

"Yes," May said over her shoulder. But she slowed down and almost immediately followed that response with, "No. We don't have to."

She came to a stop at the edge of the dock. Winnie caught up with her and watched as Reese appeared on the deck. She sobbed and grabbed May's hand. May put an arm around Winnie's waist. Reese saw them and hesitated, but then she waved to them. Winnie blew her a kiss, and May was too busy clinging to Winnie to do anything else. Reese looked amazing. She was well-rested and wearing an outfit Winnie had never seen before. A slender blonde woman was standing behind her and Winnie intuited that the stranger was a big part of how Reese had survived while she was away.

Reese disembarked and cautiously approached her sisters. Winnie left May's side, already crying as she reached out a hand to Reese.

"I'm sorry."

"No, I was wrong," Reese said. "What I did was--"

Winnie snapped, "What you did has nothing to do with it. I'm your sister. I should have acted like it. Can you ever forgive me?"

Reese's lower lip quivered. "I'll trade you. Forgiveness for forgiveness."

Winnie said, "I'll take that deal." She pulled Reese into a hug, sobbing when she felt Reese's arms tighten around her. "I'm so sorry, kiddo. I'm so sorry."

"Me too."

Winnie opened her eyes and saw the stranger watching them, trying not to, and smiling sheepishly. She wiped the tears from her eyes and squeezed Reese's waist before letting her go.

"Who is your friend?"

"This is Sarah. She helped me figure things out."

Winnie nodded to her. "Thank you, Sarah."

"You're welcome."

Reese stepped around Winnie and moved toward May as if being dragged by a magnet. May lurched forward as if afraid her twin would vanish like a mirage.

"Say something," May said. "I've never gone this long without hearing your voice. I just want to hear it again."

"Hi, Maeve."

May sobbed and took two large steps toward Reese. They hugged, kissed cheeks, and then rested their foreheads against each other. Reese put her thumbs on May's cheeks to get a good look at her and a line appeared between her eyebrows.

"May..." She dropped her voice to a whisper. "Did you have sex?"

May's cheeks flushed bright red. "You can't tell that."

"Of course I can!" She laughed and rattled May's head between her hands. "Congratulations, little girl. Was she a beauty?" May's blush deepened and Reese laughed. "Good girl. I want all the details. Every single one, okay?"

"When things have settled."

"Yeah. Definitely."

She kissed May's cheek again, a proud sister, and loosened her hold. Winnie and Sarah had moved to join them. With one hand still on May's face, Reese reached out to squeeze Winnie's shoulder. She felt more vital and awake than she ever had on the mainland. The bonds between them were already healing.

"We need to talk," Winnie said. "There was a town meeting while you were away. Jessica played her cards and I know why she's here. She wants to destroy the island. We have to figure out how to stop her. I don't think she's going to leave as quietly as she did last time."

May's expression changed slightly. "We do need to talk. But it's not as simple as you think, Arwyn."

"Looks like history does repeat itself!"

The sisters turned and saw Jessica Vaughn striding toward them. She was grinning but her eyes were set with anger. She swung her arms as she approached, then placed both fists on her hips as she stood between the Cabots and the end of the dock.

"I guess it's not really history repeating, since our positions are reversed. I think that's called poetic justice. But I don't care. I may not have fancy powers, but I can tell you what's going to happen. You three witches are going to get on that boat and leave this island. Your time here is done."

"Winnie…?" Reese looked at her older sister without moving her head.

"Winnie isn't in charge right now." May was staring hard at Jessica. "I am. We're not going to leave."

Jessica moved closer. "If I have to pick you up and put you in that boat myself…"

"No," May said. "We're not leaving. But we're not going to fight you."

Winnie said, "What?"

Reese said, "May, what're you talking about?"

May looked at her sisters. "I'm sorry I didn't have a chance to explain this to you both in private. But we're not going to fight Jessica's plan."

Jessica said, "If this is some kind of ploy—"

"No ploy," May said. "You win, Jessica."

Chapter Twenty-One

It took some convincing to get Jessica back to the Cabot house. She felt she had the upper hand, so relocating to the family's home turf looked like surrendering. Her skepticism increased when May told Winnie to retrieve their mother and grandmothers for the meeting. But May insisted there wouldn't be a fight. "We're not even going to have an argument. Not with you, anyway." She looked at her sisters with real worry. "Any fighting will be amongst family. I swear to you."

When they got back to the house, Reese hesitated on the threshold. The last time she'd been to this house, she'd been thrown out. A whole life of feeling like she belonged was erased in one act of cruel anger. She didn't realize how long she'd lingered on the porch until she felt a hand on her elbow. She looked back and saw Sarah standing at her side.

"Take your time," Sarah said softly.

Reese took Sarah's hand without looking and stepped inside. It also rankled her to have Jessica Vaughn in their house again. The last time *she'd* been there... well, it had also been a bad time. She squeezed Sarah's hand without realizing it.

"Ow. Reese..."

"Sorry. I'm sorry."

"It's okay." She adjusted her grip. "There. Squeeze as hard as you want."

They took a seat on the couch. Jessica went to the window and peered outside, pacing with her arms crossed over her chest as they waited for the final members of their little congress. May stood next to the fireplace, an awkward position to take until Reese realized she was purposefully standing in the only place where she couldn't be accused of blocking an exit. May felt her staring and looked at her. Despite her anxiety and Reese's own misgivings, they both smiled. They'd never been apart for so long in their entire lives. Just being in the same room again was like balm on a strained muscle.

"This better not be some kind of witch trap," Jessica muttered.

May closed her eyes. "Jessica, we're giving you the win. Could you please just be patient and stop trying to change my mind?"

Jessica twisted her lips into a scowl. She looked at Sarah and smiled. "Love your new girlfriend, Cerys. You tell her about our history?"

Sarah ignored the girlfriend command and calmly said, "I know all about how you went down on her and then tried to fuck her." She smiled coldly. "Didn't work out too well, I guess."

"You know she has a girlfriend here in town, too?" Jessica said. "Cheating on a married woman. Doubling down on your infidelity?"

Sarah looked at Reese. "I might not be a Cabot, but I really want someone to shut this bitch up."

"I know." Reese looked at May. "But if May says we're not going to fight, then I guess we're not going to fight. Not until we hear her game plan."

The back door opened and Ashlyn called out to her daughters as she ran into the house. "Cerys? Maeve?"

May said, "In here, Mama."

She came into the room and slammed into May without slowing down. Reese stood up and went close enough to be grabbed as well, but Winnie remained where she was. Her expression revealed that she felt too responsible for their absence to join in, but Reese held out one arm and motioned her forward.

"Come here."

"If I hadn't~"

May said, "Yeah, yeah, yeah, there's blame to go around. Get in here, Arwyn."

She joined the hug, resting her head against Reese's shoulder from behind. The hug broke up when the elder Cabots entered. Grandy scowled at May, who accepted the judgment with her chin up and shoulders squared. Ashlyn pinched May's sleeve and looked between her mother and her daughter.

"May... please. This tantrum has gone on long enough. Lift the spell you put on your grandmother. Give her voice back."

"Not until I've said what I have to say. She's not going to interrupt me."

Meemaw said, "Maeve, whatever your disagreement with her is, we can work it out. As a family. Like we always do."

"Sit down, Meemaw."

She flinched. May had never spoken to her so harshly. She looked at the couch and tilted her head in confusion when she saw Sarah.

"Who is this one?"

"She's here for Reese," Winnie said.

May cleared her throat. "Okay, now that we're all here, I want to explain everything all at once for everyone's benefit." She smoothed her hands over her skirt as the rest of the women took their seats. Jessica leaned against the wall next to the window, arms still crossed.

"The Cabot family has been part of Coventry Island from the moment it was settled. A woman from our line was the first to set foot on its soil after it rose from the sea. The island has always had power, a spirit, and that spirit asked that first ancestor to protect it. She agreed. She set up a home and waited for other travelers to find the island. When they arrived, she didn't run them off with torches. She didn't use the power given to her by the spirit to scare them so they would never return. She welcomed them. She guided the foundation of this town.

"Over the many years since that day, women with the Cabot name have stood as guardians for the island. Arwyn, Cerys, and I are the latest in that long line. We thought we were doing our job. We thought we were doing the right thing. But we were wrong. We'd been lied to." She turned and looked at Grandy. "The person who was supposed to be our mentor, who was supposed to have retired when we took on the mantle, decided we couldn't be trusted with such important work. That our sexualities made us a liability to the tradition."

Winnie said, "May, what are you talking about? We're supposed to protect the island. That's what we've been doing."

May was still looking at Grandy. "Only partially. Grandy didn't trust us. She knew about my sexuality, and Winnie's, and she knew we weren't very likely to provide offspring. That's why she suggested to Jessica to throw a wrench in everything."

Jessica had been gazing out the window, but now her attention moved back inside. "Wait, she what? I've seen this woman around town, but we've never..."

"She could have made you forget. But the point is, it was her idea. Stringing me along and then seducing Reese. She wanted to shake us up. She thought maybe if I got over my crush I would realize I don't like women after all. Right, Grandy? You of all people thought it was just a phase I could be traumatized out of. Looks like it backfired. After what happened with Jessica, I was so scared of getting close to anyone I just never tried. I never went on dates. I never approached anyone. You thought I was unlikely to have babies as a lesbian, so you scared me into staying a virgin. Well done."

Ashlyn looked at Grandy. "Mom, tell me you didn't."

May twisted her fingers. "Go ahead, Grandy. You can speak again. Use your newfound voice to lie to your own daughter."

Grandy looked at Ashlyn but quickly averted her gaze.

"She was also the one who found out Reese was having an affair with Chloe Passoth. She brought Jessica back for a second attempt at breaking up the family. She got so close." Her voice broke and she looked at her sisters. "She got Winnie and Reese to turn against each other. I never thought I would see that. But we're stronger than she gave us credit for."

Winnie said, "But why would she bring Jessica back to the island? Did she know what she's planning for the island?"

"I did," Grandy said. "I wanted Winnie to fight her alone. I wanted her to appeal to Lucas Passoth for help, a man who had just lost his wife to infidelity. I wanted them to bond through the experience. And then~"

Winnie covered her face with her hands. "Oh, for fuck's sake."

"You already have a relationship with the man. It's the only real relationship you have with anyone and it seemed like the best chance for continuing the family line."

Winnie stood up. "I'm asexual, Grandy."

"That's not a real thing."

"I feel no sexual attraction to *anyone*. Not the Jessica Vaughns or the Lucas Passoths of the world. The thought of having sex with someone is miserable to me. Would you really want to put me through that for the sake of having a baby?"

May said, "Yes. She would. A baby at any cost, a continued lineage. There have always been Cabot girls on Coventry Island, and there must *always* be Cabot girls."

Ashlyn stood up and moved toward the wall. Her only purpose seemed to be putting distance between herself and her mother. Grandy was still looking at the floor, her voice small and weak.

"The island is more important than our comfort..."

"No," May said. "You're wrong. Somewhere along the way, the message got twisted. Somewhere, someone in our family decided we had to be chained here against our will. Our promise to the island became a prison sentence. But it's not. I swear to you, Grandy, you were wrong. And by interfering with us, you almost broke the covenant."

Grandy looked up at her. "What?"

"You, Meemaw, and Mother passed the mantle to us. You were retired. Here for moral support if we needed it, but otherwise without an active role. The island is our responsibility. And ours alone." She looked at Jessica. "This is where you come in. Sorry it took a while to get to you."

Jessica said, "No apologies necessary. I've been enjoying the show."

"Our purpose was never to freeze the island in time. If it was, we would have failed every time someone built a new house or put down a road. Or, hell, put in a septic system. Our purpose was to maintain the island. To keep it alive no matter what the outside world might do to it. We've succeeded this long. The power is still flowing as powerfully as ever despite the modern touches that cropped up over the years."

She turned and walked over to where Jessica was standing.

"GreenVault. I like that name. It implies they care about the environmental impact of what they do. Is that accurate?"

Jessica still looked wary of a trick. "Yes. Actually, that's one of the reasons I wanted to work with them. They're very conscientious."

"We'll discuss their references later. If it checks out, you can count on my family's support."

The anger had faded from Jessica's face, making her look almost soft. Her eyes darted around the room as if she expected an attack, but there was real hope in her voice. "Really?"

May nodded and held out her hand. "Yes."

Jessica hesitated. Finally she uncrossed her arms and took

May's hand. "Thank you."

"It's not because of you. It's for the benefit of the whole island. We expect you to work with us to ensure the island and its energies are unharmed by the changes you wish to make. I don't like the idea of condos directly on the shoreline. But I am willing to debate with you on where they should be placed instead."

"I understand." Jessica looked confused, but she nodded. "We can have that discussion."

Winnie cleared her throat and looked at Grandy. "I'm not sure what happens now. You and Reese come home, and the three of us continue as before...?"

May looked at Reese, sadness in her eyes. "I wish that were so, Winnie. But I've had a feeling ever since I hugged Reese at the docks this morning, and it's been getting stronger the more time we spend together. She came back to the island, but her spirit is anchored elsewhere. She found a new home while she was away."

Reese tensed. "What? No. I... I just found a place to stay... temporarily..." She looked at Sarah and her voice trailed off. Sarah was looking back at her, face blank but with obvious hope in her eyes. They were still holding hands, and Reese realized she'd never even considered holding hands with either of her sisters for support.

Winnie said, "Reese...? You don't have to leave. Please."

"I know. Trust me, it's not out of anger. I swear. It's just... the work Sarah is doing in Owl Lake is so important. And she's doing it all by herself. And I love the work. She n~ the shelter needs me."

May said, "It's okay, Winnie. She can go where she's needed. The two of us can protect the island together. Or one of us... if need be."

Winnie's eyes widened. "Where am I going?"

"Nowhere. Or maybe somewhere, someday. My point is that our duty isn't what we've been told it is. We protect the island and it will protect us. If the day comes when you or I want to leave, it won't punish us. And if the day comes when we're too old or weak to continue, even if we don't have children, we can appoint someone to take on the mantle in our place."

She turned slowly and looked at all the women in the room. She smiled.

"This is what I wanted to say. The island is going to thrive, just as it always has. No matter who arrives or who goes, the island is resilient.

We've been caring for it so long that we've forgotten that it cares for us as well. It wants us to be happy. As long as there is a Cabot standing guard, this island will remain strong."

CHAPTER TWENTY-TWO

CHLOE SWUNG the door open hard enough that it rattled against the wall when she released it. She was already over the threshold, arms around Reese's neck, too distracted by her return to care about something as trivial as a door. Reese put her hands on Chloe's hips to keep them from tumbling over, but she didn't return the embrace. She closed her eyes and waited for Chloe to back up so they were face to face before she forced a smile.

"You're back. When did you get back? You look amazing. Where have you been?"

"Chloe..."

"I know. I'm rambling. But... god, I've missed you." She smoothed her hands down Reese's sleeves. "Are you okay?"

Reese said, "I'm fine."

"Lucas isn't home right now. Come in. I'll make you some tea or~"

"I'm not here to stay," Reese said. "There's something I have to tell you. I thought maybe it was clear given how our last meeting went, but I wanted to be absolutely sure. And given your greeting, it's a good thing I did. I'm sorry, Chloe, but we're finished."

Chloe's face fell. "What? Is it your sister?"

"No, it has nothing to do with them. It has to do... I was at the lowest point in my life last week. I had nowhere else to go. I came to you, and you turned me away."

"Lucas..."

Reese said, "No, I'm not asking for an explanation. I understand why you didn't let me in. I'm not saying you were wrong. I'm only saying that I can't be in a relationship where I come after a husband and a job. I love you a lot. But you're... you're... you aren't a person I can see myself ending up with. I want a relationship with forward momentum. Where we can make rules based on each other, not some third party. Maybe if I'd met you before Lucas..."

Chloe said, "Wait. Just... please, wait."

"I'm not going to talk about this, Chloe. I love you. And yes, there's a chance if we sit down and talk, you could convince me to stick around. But then what? Lucas finds out about us? I'm not waiting for someone else to decide we're over. I'm going to end this now, before it ends badly." She stepped closer and kissed Chloe between the eyebrows. "You deserve to be with someone you love more than part-time. You deserve a round-the-clock kind of love, and you can't do that until you're ready to let go of Lucas for good. You weren't willing to do that for me which means there's someone else out there waiting."

Chloe was crying. "You're the only thing that's made life bearable, Cerys."

Reese said, "That should never have been my job. You deserve a life that makes you happy, then you deserve to find someone to share that life with."

"Please don't go."

"I have to." She took Chloe's hand. "Don't let yourself be trapped in a life you don't really want. And don't settle for secret happiness, or joy that has to be stolen. What you want is out there. It's just a little scary to go looking for it."

"Reese, if you go, I'll never forgive you."

Reese smiled sadly. "I won't hold that against you. Goodbye, Chloe. Thank you for everything. I loved being with you."

She turned and stepped off the porch. She didn't look back, but judging by how long it took the door to close, Chloe had watched her depart for longer than she expected. She got to the road and stuck her hands in her pockets for the long walk home.

She'd done the right thing. It sucked and it hurt, but she knew there was no future with Chloe. She had also been surprised by May's revelations at the meeting. Not just about how Grandy had worked against them for so long, but how matter-of-factly she revealed Reese wasn't home to stay. Reese hadn't even admitted that to herself yet, but she'd felt it the entire trip from Owl Lake. It felt less like coming home and more like a pit stop.

Even now, walking from Chloe's house back home, Reese found herself looking at the town differently. That was partially due to May's... surrender? She didn't know what else to call what had happened. Jessica came back to the island with a plan of what, just one week ago, May would have called destruction. After Jessica left the house, Winnie had detailed everything that was said at the GreenVault meeting. Condos on the shore? Summer homes on the far side of the island? It made her angry just thinking about it.

But she trusted May. If she said it could be a good thing, then she was willing to lay down arms and give them the benefit of the doubt.

Winnie and May were sitting across from each other at the kitchen island when Reese got home. She moved behind Winnie's stool and wrapped both arms around her sister's shoulders, nuzzling her hair. Winnie relaxed into the embrace and swayed back and forth, hooking her fingers on Reese's arms as if she was hanging from them.

"I ended things with Chloe."

"You didn't have to."

Reese said, "No, I did. Not because of you, but because it had to end. Where's Sarah?"

May said, "She went to get something to eat. I think she could sense we wanted some time alone when you got back."

Reese pulled over a stool. She sat on the edge of the counter, between her sisters. "She's pretty intuitive like that." She folded her hands in front of her. She looked at May, then Winnie. "I guess the island isn't the only thing that's going to be overhauled."

Winnie said, "I guess not. You're really leaving?"

"Sarah needs me." She put her hand on top of May's. "The blessings we give at Stormy Mouse are great, but the shelter is a more immediate need. The clothes there will go to clothe women and children who are at their lowest point."

May smiled. "I understand. And I love the idea of you spreading our influence to the mainland. I'll miss you desperately when you're not visiting every single weekend."

Reese laughed. "I think that can probably be arranged."

Winnie put her hand on top of theirs. "And we can come down to see your new home. We can do what we can to make the shelter a truly sacred space."

"Thank you." She looked at their hands, relieved beyond words that they were together again. She knew that even if she left now it would be different. She would be choosing to leave, with full knowledge that she could come home whenever she wanted. And Owl Lake seemed infinitely closer with her sisters' blessing. She moved her other hand so she could cover Winnie's.

"So what now?" May asked.

"You tell me," Winnie said. "You seem to be doing a damn fine job steering us in the right direction."

Reese said, "Wait, first things first. Where are Grandy and Meemaw?"

"Mom took them home," Winnie said. "I get the feeling she was pretty pissed off about what May revealed, so she's going to deal with them herself. I also kind of got the feeling Grandy is washing her hands of us completely."

"Good," May said. "They've manipulated us since we were girls. If they want to cut ties, fine. But they have to come back to *us*. We won't go running to them. We can handle whatever this island throws at us without their help. It's our job."

Reese nodded.

"For now, I think we need to perform a blessing on the household. There are a lot of cracks that need healing in this family."

"Yes," Reese agreed. "I can use a nice sororal spellcasting. Indoors or out?"

"I think indoors," Winnie said. "The house needs to know we're reunited."

She slipped off the stool. Reese slipped her hand into Winnie's left, as May took the right. Winnie squeezed both hands and then led them upstairs for prayer.

Reese went to her bedroom after dinner. Sarah called them from town and asked if they wanted her to bring a meal up to the house, and they'd had an impromptu dinner party on the living room floor with fried chicken and using big serving spoons to eat the sides directly from the containers. Winnie and May told Sarah embarrassing stories from Reese's past, while Reese tried to play interference with anything too incriminating.

She looked around her room and tried to think of what she would take when she left. A lot of it could stay; she planned to be home as often as possible and she didn't want to sleep in a gutted room. She also wanted to be sure May and Winnie weren't forced to live with an emptiness in their home. She stood and went over to the baseball trophy on the dresser. She used to love baseball, but she grew out of it. She was just good enough for other kids to accuse her of using magic to get home runs. Her enjoyment of the game wasn't strong enough to make it worth the trash talk.

There was a gentle knock on the door and she turned to see Sarah in the hallway. It was strange to see the woman who'd saved her from exile standing in the family home, like sighting a celebrity in the supermarket. It was the fantastic blending with the mundane. Sarah had changed into a black-and-green plaid shirt which was untucked from her jeans.

"Sorry to disturb you," she said.

"No, it's fine." She put the trophy back down. "I'm just surprised you were able to get away from my sisters."

Sarah put her shoulder against the door. "I technically didn't. They're in Winnie's room getting something ready for me to look at."

Reese said, "I don't think they have any baby pictures of me in there…"

Sarah grinned. "No, they said something about mice…?"

"Oh. Winnie's Revolutionary War mice. They're statues. They're cute."

"Sounds like it." She casually scanned the bedroom. "So this is your childhood bedroom."

"Child- and adulthood."

"Can I come in?"

Reese nodded and Sarah crossed the threshold. She put her hands in her back pockets as she examined the pictures on the wall. "I love your sisters."

"They're great," Reese agreed, watching Sarah and fighting the urge to play tour guide. "Have you found a place to stay tonight?"

Sarah turned and looked at her. "May offered me the couch downstairs. If that's okay."

"It's perfect. It's what I was going to… well, actually, I was going to offer my bed."

"What?"

Reese blushed. "I mean, give you my bed and then *I* would take the couch. I wasn't going to imply… I mean."

"I got it," Sarah said, rescuing her. "And I suppose it's only fair, since you'll be staying with me when we go back to Owl Lake."

"I will?"

"You'll be an employee of the shelter. No need for you to keep sleeping there unless you want to. But you're more than welcome to crash at my place until you find an apartment of your own. Unless your girlfriend would find that sketchy."

"Right." She tucked her hair behind her ears. "I broke up with her today."

Sarah raised an eyebrow. "Oh. How'd that go?"

"How does that sort of thing ever go?"

"Yeah," Sarah said. "How are you?"

Reese said, "I'm okay. I'm good. I'm sad, but it's not a bad feeling. It had to happen."

"Good." Sarah moved closer. "And I feel like we should say... or at least talk about... you coming to Owl Lake. I don't want you to think I'm taking that as, uh, as an invitation to flirt with you or start anything up. Romantically."

"Oh, absolutely. I think it would be a bad idea, all things considered. The breakup being so recent. And working together."

Sarah said, "Yeah. Not that you're unattractive."

"Same to you," Reese said with an awkward laugh. "But... friends. We'll just be friends, coworkers, platonic... platonic pals."

"Right."

May appeared in the doorway. "Hey. The display is ready." She grinned. "What are you two talking about?"

"Nothing, you brat. Shoo."

May giggled as she retreated. Reese moved toward the door and Sarah followed, gesturing at the curtain between rooms as she passed it.

"This is cute. You gonna miss it when you're gone? Having your sister nearby whenever you want to talk in the middle of the night?"

Reese said, "Maybe. You might be in for a few late night conversations until I get acclimated."

"That's okay. It'll be nice to show off my pajamas. I just got a pretty cool set. They have moose on them."

"I love meese."

Sarah laughed and followed her to see Winnie's collection.

CHAPTER TWENTY-THREE

ONE YEAR, *two months, eight days later*

The sun had risen just enough to cast a shadow of the window blinds across the blankets where Sarah was still tangled in the blankets. She was facedown, her arms forming a diamond around her head where it had fallen in the crack between the pillows. Reese came into the bedroom and examined the sight, smiling before she reached down to jostle Sarah's ankle. The exposed foot turtled up under the blanket.

"Get out of bed," Reese commanded.

"Take off your pants," Sarah countered.

"I'm serious."

"So am I."

Reese continued into the bathroom to check her hair in the mirror. She was only wearing a touch of makeup; Sarah preferred to see as many of her freckles as possible, so Reese was willing to let them show. She walked back into the bedroom to see her partner hadn't moved. She crawled up on the mattress and settled on top of her. She put her lips against a layer of hair covering Sarah's left ear.

"Come on, babe. It's not like the state ferries. If we miss the boat, it probably won't go back until late this afternoon."

"So witch us over the water," Sarah suggested. "Get your flying monkeys to carry us."

Reese grabbed Sarah's sides through the blankets. Even with

the thick downy barrier, Sarah bucked and fought at the assault. "I don't have flying monkeys!"

"You do!" Sarah insisted. "Big ugly flying monkeys. And a big black pointy hat."

Reese flipped Sarah over and straddled her, glaring into her smiling face. "Everything you're saying is very, very inappropriate."

Sarah's smile wavered. "Is it? I'm sorry. I don't know when it's too far, and I'm... I was just teasing, sweetie."

"You can make it up to me by getting out of bed and getting dressed."

"Wait." She narrowed her eyes as Reese climbed off of her. "Are you really offended, or are you just using it as an excuse to guilt me into getting up?"

Reese shrugged. "Probably doesn't matter, since you're awake enough now that you might as well get out of bed no matter what."

Sarah said, "You really are evil."

"You love me, though."

"I do," Sarah admitted with a weary sigh.

Reese went into the living room. She spent the first six months of her time in Owl Lake living in a small apartment above a tailor shop. The stairs were on the outside of the building, in an alley shared by a pizza joint, and the smell forced her to have pizza or pasta for dinner much more often than she liked to admit. Sarah took her out a lot, and cooked for her, but the ease with which she could pick up a large pepperoni meant she quickly got over the novelty of living alone. When Sarah asked her to move in, she accepted immediately.

Looking back, she only regretted the time and money wasted just so she could say she'd lived by herself. The apartment was nice, but it felt more like a waiting room than a residence. She marked down the days until it was acceptable to move in with someone else. Maybe some people just needed to cohabitate. She hadn't even had a womb to herself, let alone a whole house. She needed company, she needed someone to take care of and to be there to take care of her when she felt puny.

She made Sarah's breakfast while the shower was running. By the time she appeared - fully dressed if a bit grumpy - Reese had placed her plate on the table with a fresh cup of coffee. They greeted each other properly with a kiss. Sarah checked the time on her phone.

"How fast do I have to eat?"

"You can linger. We don't have to be in Shield until ten-thirty."

Sarah put her hands flat on the table and twisted her lips, irritated. "You lied to me about when we had to leave?"

Reese held up a hand, thumb and forefinger pinched close together. "This way we can be leisurely about it. A nice slow breakfast. Fill up on gas. No hurry."

"God, you're awful."

"But you're still with me."

"For some reason."

Reese grinned and took a bite of her eggs. "People have gotten married for less."

Sarah narrowed her eyes and chewed carefully. "We're still a little early for married. How about engaged? You can call off an engagement without everyone losing their minds. And that will give us time to prepare for a wedding. Should there be one."

"Sort of like putting something under the counter before you buy. Not that I buy into the marriage-as-property thing."

"Of course," Sarah said, "and yeah. Like a probationary period. If we don't get sick of each other by the wedding date, we'll go through with it."

Reese held her hand out across the table. Sarah rubbed her fingertips on a napkin - she made a steeple out of them and then rubbed back and forth instead of wiping, an adorable affectation Reese loved - and reached out to shake on it.

"I think you're in trouble, though. We've had fights where I hated your guts but I still loved you."

"When did you hate my guts?"

Reese rolled her eyes. "I'm not going to give examples. But the point is, even then, I knew I'd probably stick around if you let me."

Sarah made a non-committal noise and poked at her food. They finished eating, put away the dishes, and checked to make sure they had everything before leaving. At the door, Sarah pulled Reese back into the house and kissed her passionately. Reese muttered in surprise, swaying from one foot to the other, and resting her hand on the back of Sarah's head until the kiss ended. Sarah twisted to whisper in Reese's ear.

"I'm crazy about you. You know that, right?"

"It's the only reason I let you get away with saying such mean things." She smiled and squeezed Sarah just below the belt, making her squeal. "C'mon. May's going to be mad if we're late."

Sarah linked fingers with Reese on the way to the car. "If we get married, will that make me a Cabot?"

"Only if you take my name."

"But will it give me... I mean, will I be like you and your sisters?"

Reese stopped and considered the question. "My grandmother-by-marriage became like us, but she actually lives on the island. We'd be coming back to live here, with no other Cabots in the vicinity to help you learn. You might get a little tickle of power, but you wouldn't be like me and my sisters. Sorry."

"It's okay. I'm fine with you being the magic one in the relationship."

"Well, you've obviously never seen yourself fresh out of the shower. Talk about magical..."

Sarah laughed.

They arrived in Shield with plenty of time to spare. Sarah bought a can of DuChilly nuts for the sisters, an unnecessary peace offering since Winnie and May both adored her, while Reese stood on the dock and watched ship slowly approach. Sarah moved up silently beside her and linked their fingers together, watching her as a smile spread across her features.

"You miss it, don't you? Home."

"Home is Owl Lake," Reese said. "I know you, Sarah, and I know you're about to say we can talk about moving to the island when we get married. But I don't want that, no matter how much I miss it." She turned to face Sarah fully. "That might be where I started and it will always be where I'm from, but you're my home. You're where I'm going."

Sarah put her hands on Reese's shoulders. "Marry me."

"We did this at breakfast."

"No, we did a bit at breakfast. You deserve to be asked for real."

Reese smiled. "Then you deserve a real answer. Yes, Sarah, I'll marry you."

They were still kissing when the boat arrived. Barty came off the bridge and whistled through his teeth at them. "Y'all cut that out, now. Disgusting."

Reese said, "I'm surprised at you, Barty. Disgusted by the sight of two women kissing?"

He snorted. "I don't want to see *anyone* kissing you, Cerys Cabot. You and your sisters are all twelve years old and always will be in my eyes. No more of that smooching stuff or I'll tell your mama."

Reese laughed and pecked his cheek as she walked onboard. Sarah sat next to her on one of the benches which ringed the deck. Barty waited for other travelers, watching as a few cars loaded themselves up in the underside of the ship. When the ferry lanes were empty, he blew his horn as a warning to any stragglers he was about to leave. Sarah checked her watch.

"That's twenty-two minutes I could have spent sleeping."

"What, you kept track?"

"Mm-hmm. For next time."

Reese guided Sarah's head to her shoulder and let her doze for the short trip to the island. When they got closer she twisted to look behind her, watching the town roll slowly into view. Her heart jumped when she saw the skeletal outlines of construction projects on the shore. May had convinced her, convinced the entire town, that voting for GreenVault was the right thing to do. Jessica and Lucas began planning as soon as the measure passed.

She trusted her sister. She did. But trusting it was the right thing and actually witnessing the construction on an otherwise pristine shore were two very different things. In her heart, she felt like they'd dropped the walls and were allowing the enemy to set up camp in their home.

"Hey."

Reese looked at Sarah, who was staring at her. Sarah brushed the back of her finger over Reese's cheek.

"It's change. Change is supposed to be scary and weird."

"Thank you." Reese kissed the corner of Sarah's mouth. "It's just... my home."

Sarah nodded. "The high school I went to was bulldozed a year after I graduated. The new one was exquisite. The Drama kids actually got a theater where they could put on plays, and the classes were more spacious. There was a parking lot which actually had enough spaces for every student to park. But I hated it. I thought it was an eyesore because it wasn't mine."

Reese said, "What made you change your mind?"

"Who said I did? I hope that piece of shit is destroyed by a freak earthquake next summer."

Reese laughed and kissed her. "You're the best thing that's ever happened to me."

Sarah said, "You're joking, right? You're the gift. One day you come wandering up to the shelter out of the blue. You offer to give me a hand, you take the weight off my shoulders. You can do magic. I loved going to work every day but at the same time it was killing me. You were a godsend." There were tears in her eyes. "I'm just fortunate you also think I'm hot, because I could not deal with an unrequited crush situation."

Every qualm Reese had about leaving the island, no matter how minor, evaporated. She kissed Sarah and then stood, taking her hand to move closer to the ramp so they could disembark immediately upon arrival. From their perspective it felt as if they were standing still while Coventry Island rolled into position to welcome them. Reese took the hand of her fiancé and led her onto solid ground.

May had been working with Jessica and GreenVaults' executives to ensure the environmental impact was minimal. True to the company's word, they seemed eager for her input. Winnie was cautiously optimistic, so Reese was as well. As for Winnie, the bakery was thriving. Construction crews and representatives from GreenVault created a flood of new customers for her. She was bulking up her savings because she wanted to buy Will & Winn from Lucas Passoth free and clear.

Which brought her mind back to Chloe. When the GreenVault project got underway, Lucas' attention to business went into overdrive. It turned out that he'd never had an affair; Jessica was the mystery woman, and his secretive behavior was because he didn't want word of the partnership to get out before everything was official. A few months after Reese moved off the island, he asked Chloe for a divorce. She granted it in exchange for full ownership of the garage. He agreed and the two parted ways amicably. Chloe sold the garage for a profit and moved off the island. She and Reese occasionally touched base via email. Last she heard, Chloe was working at a garage in Shepherd, a town just north of Seattle. She'd met a woman. They were moving slowly, but she sounded extraordinarily happy.

Sarah stopped walking when they reached the supermarket. "I'm going to get some groceries. I don't want to mooch off your sisters all weekend."

"Translation, you want to give me some time alone with my sisters."

"A shopping trip can have two purposes." Sarah smiled and kissed her. "Say hello to them for me."

"I will." She smoothed Sarah's hair once more, then released her.

Sarah went inside and Reese continued up the street, hands in her pockets unless she had to return the wave of someone who spotted her. She might have left but she certainly wasn't forgotten. When she reached the corner she stopped to look up at their grandmothers' house. Things had changed for the worse there. Grandy still thought she'd been doing the right thing, protecting the island at all costs, and she refused to apologize for everything she'd done. Meemaw was standing with her, which meant none of the girls had spoken to them for months. A senior outreach program took care of their meals now, so May didn't have to trek up every night to cook dinner. Ashlyn was stuck in the middle but sided with her daughters. She'd been the third person to cast a vote for GreenVault - Reese and Winnie were the first - to show everyone else on the island they truly did believe it was the right thing to do.

She waved to the house and continued walking. She believed May was right. Time marched on. Normalcy was safe and comfortable and, sometimes, the scary road was exactly the one you needed to take.

Winnie and May were sitting on the roof when Reese approached. May lifted both hands over her head in an enthusiastic greeting, while Winnie settled for a one-handed wave while her other hand gripped May's dress to keep her from tumbling off the house. Reese bounced on the balls of her feet and closed the distance in a run, slamming open the front door and taking the stairs two at a time. She went through her old bedroom (still decorated, but with a larger bed for Sarah's comfort) and crawled through the open window. Winnie and May scooted apart to give her room. She hugged Winnie, gave May three kisses on the cheek, and then grabbed both of their hands.

"Welcome home," May said.

"We've missed you," Winnie said.

Reese brought their hands to her mouth and kissed their fingers. "I missed you, too."

"Where's the pretty half of your relationship?" Winnie asked.

"Hey!" May snapped. "We're twins!"

"Sororal twins," Winnie said. "I'm not insulting *your* looks. You didn't get any of those ugly freckles."

Reese glared at May. "You let her get nasty while I was gone."

"Why are you mad at me?!" May shrieked.

Reese laughed and leaned against her twin. "Sarah is at the store picking up a few necessities. She wanted to give us time to get reacquainted."

Winnie nodded. "I like her."

"Me too," May said.

"Good. It would be bad for you to hate your sister-in-law."

They both looked at her, then at each other, making sure they hadn't misheard before they shrieked and crushed Reese in their hug.

"Let. Go. Of me!" Reese demanded, fighting weakly. "We haven't even set the date yet. We just decided this morning."

Winnie kissed Reese's cheek. "You're going to be so happy with her. She's perfect for you, Reese." May was nodding her agreement. "Congratulations, babe."

"Thank you," Reese said, suddenly shy.

The three pulled away from each other. May leaned back on her hands. Winnie wrapped her arms around herself in a hug. Reese pulled her feet up so they were flat against the shingles and rested her arms on her knees. They could see the construction on the shore, but it didn't obstruct their view of the water or the docks. Reese could see Barty moving around on the dock of his ship as clearly as ever. Downtown had more people, yes, but it didn't look overly crowded and the noise level was the same. Maybe there would be crowds when construction was finished, maybe there wouldn't be. Maybe there were unforeseen problems lurking that wouldn't be noticeable until years down the road.

Reese could be patient. Whatever problems the island might face someday, it would find the Cabot girls waiting to knock it down. There had always been Cabot girls on Coventry Island, fighting to protect it, standing strong against those who might do it harm.

And there always would be.

ABOUT THE AUTHOR

Geonn Cannon lives in Oklahoma. He is the author of several novels, including the Riley Parra series which is now a webseries for Tello Films, and an official Stargate SG-1 tie-in novel. Information about his other novels and an archive of free stories can be found online at geonncannon.com.

"Riley Parra is a strong, badass heroine for those that like their coffee and their cop fiction bitter." - P Industry

No Man's Land isn't the kind of place you go after dark, even if you have a badge. But Detective Riley Parra was born there, and she refuses to surrender it to the drug dealers, killers and criminals who have made it there home. The case of a body stuffed into a drainage pipe leads her to discover that there is far more at stake than she ever imagined.

   ~ Riley Parra, Season One

"A good novel to while away a few hours in front of the fire." - Kitty Kat Reviews

Three years ago, Sofia Kennedy reported the tragic death of her girlfriend live-on air. Still in the closet even with her closest friends, she was forced to suffer her loss in silence. In the years since she's become isolated and sticks strictly to a routine that prevents her from encountering painful memories of the woman she lost.

Marion Vogt runs a small but well-respected catering service that feeds the elite of Seattle. When Sofia's consumer reporting segment does a story on Marion's company, the two women immediately butt heads. An unintended insult results in a scathing report that nearly shuts down the business. Marion's attempt to defend herself results in a deepening of their conflict until both women are ready to destroy one another.

They quickly find out Seattle can be a very small town when trying to avoid someone. As much as they want to avoid each other, fate keeps forcing Sofia and Marion to cross paths. Before long they realize they'll have to decide if they're going to hold on to bad feelings or risk forgiveness to discover just what they have to offer each other.

   ~ Breaking Anchor